Prince
Ever
After

A.C. ARTHUR

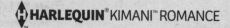

HARLEQUIN® KIMANI™ ROMANCE

London Borough of Hackney	
91300001053926	
Askews & Holts	
AF ROM	£6.50
	5596840

ISBN-13: 978-0-373-86505-5

Prince Ever After

Copyright © 2017 by Artist Arthur

♦ HARLEQUIN®
™ www.Harlequin.com

Printed in U.S.A.

A.C. Arthur is an award-winning author who lives in Baltimore, Maryland, with her husband and three children. An active imagination and a love for reading encouraged her to begin writing in high school, and she hasn't stopped since.

Books by A.C. Arthur

Harlequin Kimani Romance

Second Chance, Baby
Defying Desire
Full House Seduction
Summer Heat
Sing Your Pleasure
Touch of Fate
Winter Kisses
Desire a Donovan
Surrender to a Donovan
Decadent Dreams
Eve of Passion
One Mistletoe Wish
To Marry a Prince
Loving the Princess
Prince Ever After

Visit the Author Profile page
at Harlequin.com for more titles.

To all the dreamers.

Chapter 1

The breeze cut across his face like a million tiny pin-pricks. Beneath him the engine purred like a satisfied female as the wheels smoothly took on another sharp turn on a road where there was only one lane's worth of space.

He'd traveled this road so many times before and most times at the same rate of speed. His fingers hugged the steering wheel in an easy embrace, his back and body comfortable against the smooth leather seats of the silver-metallic Jaguar XJ220. Night had fallen over the mountains and cliffs of the island an hour ago, and he'd itched to get out of the confines of his everyday dress clothes and the formal dining room of the royal palace. It reminded him of his teenage years. Prince Roland Simon DeSaunters tossed his head back and laughed.

He'd been such a hellion back then. But eleven years ago didn't seem that long, surely not long enough for him to mature into the prince that everyone expected him to be. He'd had too long to practice being reckless, adventurous and fearless, to bottle all that spirit and simply sit still as a member of the royal family of Grand Serenity Island. That wasn't Roland's speed at all.

His speed was fast. Fun. Borderline rowdy.

With that thought, he took another curve, going downhill as he headed into town. The moment he'd been able to escape the clutches of another tension-filled family dinner, Roland had climbed into his car and driven to the small house hidden in the clefts of the mountainside that he adored. It had been his first major purchase the moment he'd been old enough to spend a part of his inherited fortune without adult supervision. The house was a high school graduation gift to himself, although he hadn't actually been able to live in it until his four years in the Royal Seaside Navy had been completed. His place was located on the southern tip of the island, where construction had not yet reached. Therefore, this part of his homeland was still flanked with dense forestation. Two of the island's tallest mountains dubbed the Serene Mountains for their location thrust through the greenery.

Roland loved it here. The scent of the tropical air rejuvenated him. The stretch of the empty road encouraged him. This was where Roland thrived and very few people knew about it. Of course, there were guards here, he was a prince, after all. But he did not keep a formal staff, preferring to do for himself when he was there. That was the reason he drove himself tonight. He had an important appointment to keep and so he pressed harder on the gas and made yet another sharp turn, smiling into the breeze as his car handled perfectly.

Fifteen minutes later Roland pulled into a dark alley. He parked his car alongside a white stone dwelling. He got out and took the steps two at a time, until he reached a door that was painted a vibrant orange. Windows climbing up the front and back walls of the building had bright white borders and orange window boxes with flowers pouring out of each one.

A slender woman answered after he knocked on the door once. She stood quietly as Roland stepped inside. The hallway was narrowand he walked slowly, anticipation bubbling in his blood. The tips of his fingers tingled and his mind emptied of anything and everything that could be a distraction.

That included the attacks on his family that had resulted in the royal palace being on lockdown for the past six months. The palace had even stopped having guests, and any staff member who hadn't been vetted, questioned and watched on a daily basis was dismissed.

His father's wedding would take place in just four weeks. His father's fiancée was one royal pain in the ass. His older brother, Kris, was married and still worried about a few accounts at their family bank. His sister, Sam, was married and glowing with love—she'd begun turning over the majority of her responsibilities on the island to Landry, his sister-in-law. And, of course, Malayka, the pain-in-the-ass soon-to-be princess.

Roland pushed all of that out of his mind. He focused instead on red and black, diamonds, hearts, clubs and spades.

"We thought you might have changed your mind."

That was the first comment that greeted Roland after he'd cleared the steps and walked down a short hallway into a brightly lit room. The walls were painted white there, too, and were covered in framed pictures of children, teenagers and older people. All photos had been taken on Grand Serenity, all faces appeared happy and content.

The round table in the center of the room had six chairs surrounding it, one of them empty.

"Game time is at nine," Roland replied and looked at the Harry Winston Ocean Tourbillon watch he wore. "It's eight fifty-five."

"In the nick of time," a second man spoke as Roland made his way to the empty chair and took a seat.

The first man who had spoken was Nelson Magloo, a fifty-something-year-old man who favored fedora hats and gold pinkie rings. Last year, Magloo and his twenty-one-year-old wife, Isla, had built a mansion on the eastern side of the island. Magloo was an oil tycoon from Nevada who'd just recently found out he'd inherited stock in the old Chapman oil refinery on the island.

The second man to speak was Henri Jauvian, a French businessman vacationing on the island in secret with one of his many mistresses.

Also in attendance were Reece McCallum, famed NASCAR driver; Kip Sallinger, owner of the Moonlight Casino; and Hugo Harrington, one of Roland's father's oldest friends. The group had been assembled by invitation only and Roland was honored to join them.

He would also be honored to take every dime they each brought to the table.

"Who's dealing?" he asked when they all continued to stare at him.

"That's right," Reece remarked with a crooked grin. "Can't expect the royal prince to deal the cards for us."

"I can deal cards just fine," Roland told him. "Just as I can take your money without a second's hesitation."

"Cocky bastard, ain't he?" Kip said with a chuckle that made his rotund upper body vibrate.

"But he can't play no better than his granddaddy could," Hugo added and took another puff on his cigar.

Roland was used to cigar smoke. His father kept a humidor on his desk and two in his private suite. Rafferty DeSaunters loved few things in life, his children and his cigars being among them.

"Josef couldn't play worth squat," Hugo continued after the cards had been dealt.

Roland held his cards loosely as he sat back in the chair. "And yet, he beat your father and a much younger, healthier and cockier you, on more than one occasion."

The others laughed and Hugo frowned. "I won plenty. My pappy, well, he was another story," Hugo quipped. "Now pony up fools. I'm in for three."

Reece whistled. "Three thousand dollars. Hugo, you hit the lottery or somethin'?"

"No lottery here on the island. Good ole Rafe don't like gamblin' too much. I was surprised as the rest of the islanders when he let you come down here and open up that big shiny casino," Hugo said to Kip.

Roland remained silent as he continued to contemplate the cards in his hand.

He didn't comment on the subject at hand because he knew how his father felt about gambling. Roland's sitting there at this very moment had a lot to do with Rafe's misgivings on the subject. The DeSaunters family history, where gambling was concerned, was no secret, no matter how much Rafe wished it were.

Josef Marquise DeSaunters was not only known for leading the revolt against Marco Vansig and thus taking control of Grand Serenity in the late 1950s, but for his luck with the cards. Before the plan to take back the island had ever entered Josef's mind, he was a hustler. Or, at least, that's what Roland liked to think, because a good high-stakes card game was not the only venture that his grandfather excelled at. Josef could talk a woman out of her fortune. With his root-beer-colored eyes and movie-star looks, Josef would likely have the woman naked in bed while at the same time be emptying her bank account. He was good-looking, charismatic, fun-loving and, above all, courageous. All traits Roland felt blessed to possess himself. On more than one occasion he'd wondered what it would have been like to be Josef's son, instead of Rafe's.

Rafferty DeSaunters walked the straight line. He made the right decisions, did the honorable thing, said the perfect words and fought the good battle. He was, in every sense of the word, born to be a prince. Roland, on the other hand, was not. Or, at least, that's what the press said.

Roland set his cards facedown on the table, reached into the inside pocket of his jacket and pulled out a wad of cash. He counted until he'd matched Hugo's amount.

"I'm in," he said somberly and placed the remaining bills back inside his jacket.

"Yeah, I'm just feelin' lucky tonight. Real damn lucky," Hugo said.

Hugo held his cards tight and was grinning as if he knew he held the winning hand. Roland almost smiled at that thought. Instead, he remained silent, watching as the others studied their cards and made their moves. There had been no reason to go over the rules for this game; they'd all played at this level before. The secret, all cash, no-holds-barred level. There would also be no tell signs, Roland thought as he looked across the table to Reece, who was still studying what he'd been dealt. They were all professionals, which meant each one of them was just as good at bluffing as he was at winning. At least, four of them were.

"Fold," Henri said grimly and pushed his cards face-down toward the deck.

Kip and Reece added their bets to the pot, and Hugo smiled giddily. "Yes sir! Lucky indeed!"

Reece put down two cards, nudging them toward the dealer so he could take two new ones. Kip took one new card. Hugo took none. Neither did Roland.

"I'll raise the bet," Hugo said, "to three thousand five hundred."

Roland was amused.

Reece folded. Kip did, too.

Roland saw the bet.

Hugo continued to smile.

Roland slowly set his cards down faceup in a neat row on the table.

Hugo almost fell out of his chair he was so excited. A huge grin spread across the man's face as he fanned himself with his cards. "Best night ever!" he said before finally dropping his cards to the table.

Roland didn't look down to see his opponent's cards immediately. Instead, he kept his gaze trained on Hugo Harrington. He was a short man, well below Roland's six-foot-one-inch stature. He had a very round face with a dusky-brown complexion. When he laughed, his chins, all three of them, shook in a funny, animated way. His bugged eyes watered and the thick, bristly mustache above his top lip twitched. Something wasn't right.

"You're an idiot, Harrington," Kip stated. "Your hand's a loser."

Reece chuckled as he reached over and spread Hugo's cards farther apart. "Yeah, man, you lost. And His Royal Highness over here only has three of a kind. He beat you with a royal bluff."

Roland still did not look down at the cards. He continued to stare at Hugo, who continued to laugh.

"Oh, he won, alright. He won the best prize ever!" Hugo told Roland. "See this right here?"

Hugo had reached into the money pot, sifting through the bills he'd thrown down. "This here, this little slip of paper, is a promissory note."

"What?" Kip asked. "You put up the money for the bet. Why add a promissory note in, too? Have you been drinking, old man?"

Hugo shook his head, one tear running down his face as he continued to chuckle. "It's fake. All of it is fake! Got it from some sailor a few months ago. Should have known the bastard was crooked from the start. Who the hell would pay all that money for one of Val's pictures? Just ridiculous!"

"You tryin' to cheat us old man?" Reece asked. "We play an honorable game here."

Now Hugo was standing and nodding. "I know. I know. The prince, especially, is honest and loyal. All of the DeSaunters are. Ain't that correct?" he asked with another nod.

Roland was feeling uneasy now. Actually, he was quite irritated.

"I got your winnings, though," Hugo told him. "I got the payment you deserve. Don't you worry. Come on, follow me."

Reece and Kip looked at Roland questioningly. Roland didn't hesitate, but stood and followed the old man down a short hall.

"I wouldn't cheat you, Your Highness. No, not at all. I'm an honorable man, too. Just like my daddy before me and his before him. We've been on Grand Serenity since the beginning and we do what's right. We keep our word," Hugo told him. "Unlike others."

Hugo said the last word as he turned the knob on a door at the end of the hallway.

"Your prize, Prince Roland," Hugo said, and motioned for Roland to enter.

The scream that greeted Roland before he could even take a step was ear shattering. The curses that followed were fluent and angry.

The half-dressed woman spouting the saucy words was…for lack of a better word…impressive.

Why had she let her father borrow her car? Why had she agreed to stay at his house tonight while he went out on yet another crazy chase for fortune and fame? Why, oh why, was this her life?

Valora "Val" Harrington had asked herself these questions over and over as she reached for her bag and began to change out of the uniform she wore while working as a tour guide at the Serenade Museum. She'd worked there for the last three years in lieu of pursuing her dream to become an artist. But that was only partially true. Val *was* an artist. Her paintings were far better than a good number of the ones hanging in the museum. The only things she was missing were an agent and high-paying clients clamoring over them.

She'd settled for the job at the museum because it was the closest thing she had to the life she really wanted. Grand Serenity was her home. She'd been born there and had never entertained the thought of leaving the beautiful island. She could paint in the evenings in the comfort of her home, but during the day she shared the history and the artifacts of her heritage. It was a complete picture, even if deep down she wished for something more.

On the other hand, her father, Hugo Harrington, was a totally different subject, one Val had been struggling with her entire life. Her mother had died in childbirth. Val was Hugo's only child. His only daughter. That hadn't been Hugo's plan. He'd wanted sons to carry on the Harrington name, to stand next to the royal family in the place he'd always thought was owed him thanks to his father's contributions to the battle that put the DeSaunters family in the palace.

It was an old story, one that Hugo had told Val over and over while Val was growing up. It was also the reason Hugo drank and gambled more than he had ever worked to support Val. It was a good thing Val had been a cute child and that one of the women her father had fallen into bed with had worked for a beauty pageant. From the time Val was six years old until her sixteenth birthday, she and her father had lived comfortably on her winnings from being a participant in one pageant after another.

But by the time she was sixteen, Val was done. She had refused to do another pageant. That was nine years ago. Her father had continued to drink, curse, gamble and guilt-trip her ever since.

Now, he was smiling as Val held a pillow over her chest and glared at him and the man that he'd just escorted into the room. The man who was the prince of this beautiful island she called home.

"What are you doing? I thought you were going to be out tonight. Why are you…why is he…what are you doing?" she exclaimed. Hugo, who looked as proud as a peacock, dressed in an appropriately colorful shirt and ragged black jeans, grinned.

"Here's your winnings," Hugo replied clapping his beefy hand onto the prince's shoulder. "She's a beauty, isn't she? I mean, really she is. Got all the pageant prizes to say so. Now, I know what you're thinking…"

To Val's complete mortification, her father continued to talk, his words oddly clear even though she could smell the liquor oozing from his pores from across the room.

"Sure, she was promised to Prince Kristian. But he's all married up now to that American. So there's no harm, no foul here. You can have her and this'll settle our debt," Hugo announced with another smile.

"Dad!" Val yelled. "Are you crazy?"

He ignored her, something he'd been doing for most of her life. Despite sharing his DNA, Val never really felt like his daughter. More often than not, she was his commodity.

"Get out! I want both of you to get out!" she screamed.

The window behind her was open and a warm breeze blew in, reminding her that she only wore her work pants, shoes and a bra. The pillow in front of her was certainly large enough to keep her covered, but still, she was standing there in her bra. She was so angry her hands were beginning to shake and she thought for one instant that she might actually lose her grip on the pillow and then...what? She would be flashing the prince of Grand Serenity. And, as if that wasn't bad enough, she was wearing her old cotton bra with the broken snap in the back. Yeah, this was the perfect Friday night scenario.

"I apologize, ma'am," the prince said before giving her a slight bow and then turning to her father. "I'll speak to you outside, Harrington."

The prince walked out of the room but her father stayed. "Put some clothes on and come out to meet the prince. You're embarrassing me," he said in what was supposed to be a whisper, but Val was certain everyone in the vicinity could hear his drunken words.

She made a sound that was animalistic, which was all that she could muster. She was so freakin' angry. She was embarrassed as hell, too, but the anger was really trying to take over.

The minute that door closed, Val grabbed her work shirt and shoved her arms back through the openings.

She buttoned it hastily and grabbed her purse and bag. When she opened that door minutes later it was, thankfully, to an empty hallway. Her feet couldn't seem to carry her outside fast enough. A short way down the street she saw her car and hustled to it as quickly as she could. She stopped at the driver's-side door and cursed again when she remembered her father had her car keys.

"I can drive you home."

No, no, no, she chanted silently without turning around.

"Your father can't find your keys. He's looking, but I doubt he'll be successful. At least, not until he's a bit more sober."

Realizing that it was rude to keep her back turned to a member of the royal family, Val turned slowly. She looked up into soft brown eyes and sighed.

"I'm sorry," she said to him. "I'm sure this is not how you expected to spend your Friday night."

Roland DeSaunters was known for the gambling, partying and womanizing that had earned him the Reckless Royal title. Standing on the street offering a ride to a museum worker had to be a far stretch from entertainment to him.

"I can walk home," she told him.

"No. You cannot," he replied. His gaze had gone down to her chest and back up to her face.

A quick glance down showed that she'd buttoned her shirt wrong, so that the material was now lopsided with a gap that proudly displayed a good swatch of her sensible white bra.

Groaning, Val turned away from him. "I can. I will.

And I'll be fine. Thank you and good night, Your Highness."

His hand on her arm was a shock—first, because he was the prince and all that royal business. But second, because the quick jolt of heat that had moved from her wrist up to her arm quickly spread across her chest.

"I cannot let you walk home at this time of night," he said when he came around to once again stand in front of her. "My car is just up the hill. I'll carry your bag while we walk and then I'll take you home."

When Val opened her mouth to speak, he simply shook his head.

"Do you really want to add to your father's embarrassing circumstances by refusing the prince?"

She did not. So Val clamped her lips shut and let him slide the bag from her shoulder. She folded her arms and walked beside him, hating every mortifying step she had to take because of her father.

Chapter 2

Second only to the royal palace, the Serenade Museum on Grand Serenity Island was a work of art all by itself. No matter how many times Val walked through the corridors of the ensemble of buildings set apart from the island's Main Street by a stone bridge and its own surrounding water, she marveled at its intricate beauty.

"The Sunset is the largest of the four buildings that make up the Serenade Museum." Val spoke to a group of twenty-five tourists. "Each building, as well as the main idea for the museum were designed by Princess Vivienne DeSaunters. These domed ceilings and the circular layout were incorporated after Vivienne had taken a trip to Berlin and became in awe of their museum island."

One of the guests raised her hand and stated, "She

was from Sugar Land, Texas. My family lives just down the road from the house where her grandparents and parents once lived."

Val smiled and quietly acknowledged the woman's heavy accent as she spoke proudly.

"Yes, the late Princess Vivienne was from America. She was very proud of her heritage and wanted to bring that same pride to the people of Grand Serenity by showcasing pieces of art that told the story of our island's beginnings," Val informed them.

"As we continue to this area," she continued while leading the group through an arched opening. "We'll see the Numismatic Collection which consists of coins that were pulled from the depths of the Caribbean Sea. In the late 1600s, after this island was acquired by the Netherlands, they were plagued by pirates and thus had to defend the island before life here could really begin to flourish. These coins," she said as she motioned toward the glass-encased counters, "were actually part of several pirates' booty. They pay homage to the Golden Age of Piracy which lasted from 1690 to 1730."

"Will the new princess continue to approve funding for the museum?"

Val turned quickly at the odd question and looked up to see it had come from the same woman with the accent.

"Rumors back in the States say she has a plan to completely overhaul and update this island," the woman continued while keeping eye contact with Val.

It was like a challenge, Val thought. Or was it? She didn't know because she'd never been faced with a tourist who knew more than she did about any topic in this museum. To be completely fair, Malayka Sampson was not a topic at the museum. At least, not until she was actually married to Prince Rafferty. With that in mind, Val decided to proceed with caution. The last thing she wanted to be accused of doing was adding to gossip about a soon-to-be member of the royal family.

"We are all anticipating the royal wedding," Val told them.

She smiled and was just about to walk to another display, which held more coins, when another tourist spoke up.

"There have been two royal weddings within months of each other. I would say love is definitely in the air here on Grand Serenity," the much younger woman with a brilliant smile said as she elbowed the handsome guy next to her.

Val nodded. "I think you could say that. Prince Kristian and Princess Landry are very happy and the new princess is making astounding contributions to the island already. As for Princess Samantha and her husband, Gary, they continue to dedicate their time and talents to the island, as well. The DeSaunters family has always been loyal and dedicated to Grand Serenity."

"Do you think the Reckless Royal will ever marry?" the now-familiar woman with the accent asked.

A man chuckled. "Hell, no! Not if he knows what's good for him. He's gonna get way more play from the ladies as a single prince than if he ties himself down with one woman."

"Huh! I doubt that," the younger woman argued. "Ever heard of gold diggers and home wreckers?"

Murmurs came from the crowd. More opinions, Val supposed, that didn't involve the museum or her job.

Her head was beginning to hurt. After three earlier tours, this was the last one of the day and she really wanted it to be over with so she could go home, take a hot bath and settle in for the night. She did not want to stand there and fend off rumors or make assumptions about the royal family, or anyone else, for that matter.

"Ever heard of falling in love? Cherishing your wife? Respecting the covenant of marriage?" Yet another woman asked. "I swear, all young people think about these days are one-night stands and monetary compensation for time served in a relationship."

"The woman that puts up with Roland DeSaunters's gambling and philandering should damn well be compensated big-time! Did you see how much money he lost in a poker game just last month? And then the two women he was seen coming out of that hotel in Dubai with?" This woman shook her head in disgust. "He's gonna be a slippery snake to tame."

"Awww, come on. I wouldn't say all that."

Val's head shot up at the sound of his voice. She had to come up on tiptoes to see over the heads of the people in her group. Seconds after he spoke, the crowd parted like the royal horns were blowing to signal a procession. And there he stood, amidst people who had paid seventy-five dollars per person to tour the island's famed museums. Prince Roland DeSaunters was dressed in a black suit and a white collarless shirt. A colorful reflection bounced off the silver watch at his wrist, thanks to the sun's vibrant rays drifting through the large arched windows.

When nobody spoke again, he walked down the aisle the people had created, coming to a stop beside Val. She had swallowed a number of times in an attempt to find her voice. As the tour guide, she should say something. That was a given. But what exactly was she supposed to say? It wasn't every day that the prince appeared and inserted himself into a tour.

"The present is always a juicier topic of discussion than the past," the prince said to the crowd. "Wouldn't you agree, Ms. Harrington?"

"That's it!" the first woman with all the questions about Malayka shouted. "I knew I recognized your face from somewhere. You're Valora Harrington. You were engaged to Prince Kristian before he dumped you for an American."

And now her mortification was complete.

Not only had seeing Roland again brought back the infuriating memories of last night and her father's foolish bet, now this woman was touching on yet another embarrassing subject for her. Would it ever end?

"The prince and I were never engaged," Val stated evenly. "As the time for arranged marriages has long since come and gone here, the union that was envisioned by my father was highly overrated."

"In other words," Roland added with his standard drop-the-panties smile, "my brother was never committed to any relationship with this woman and therefore could not have been so foolish as to dump her for someone else."

Val felt the heat rising immediately. It crept up her neck and filled her face until she almost gasped with the thought that she was actually blushing.

"Now," Roland continued with a snap of his fingers. "Let's move on to more exciting stories. Like the time I found one of these doubloons in an old trunk at the palace. It was quite a find, and my siblings were sick with jealousy because I found it instead of them."

He talked so easily as he walked casually through the marble-floored rooms. The tourists, thankfully, jumped right into his tale of treasure discoveries in the royal palace and the possibility of more being left about the island. Val wondered if he knew he had a natural gift for storytelling. That was what he was doing, she thought about twenty minutes later when they were finishing the tour and Roland was coming to a grand finish complete with a tattered map that was said to have belonged to the infamous pirate Blackbeard.

There had been no need for her to say a word since Roland had covered not only The Sunset building, but The Starlight building, as well. For the latter, he had woven a bit of romantic intrigue into his story, while highlighting some pieces from the antiquities collection and the island's early history collections.

Now they were once again coming to stand beneath the domed ceiling in the front entryway. It was about half an hour before closing, so there were other customers milling about this area, as well. When she overheard a member of the group asking if the tour was over, Val remembered she was actually supposed to be working and cleared her throat.

"Let's give Prince Roland a hand for the wonderful tour he's hosted for us this afternoon," she said and began clapping so that the group members would follow suit.

Roland looked at her and then back to the crowd, but Val did not continue to stare at him. Instead, she moved through her closing soliloquy.

"The gift shop is open for one hour after the museum actually closes, so please feel free to head in that direction. As it's nearing dinnertime, may I suggest taking the island trolley over to the northern side of the island where restaurants and other nightlife spots are open and waiting to serve and entertain you. If you're staying on the island for a few days, there's a candlelight dinner boat ride at the port tomorrow evening. And, for younger guests, there will be face painting and a magic show on Main Street beginning tomorrow at noon. We thank you and appreciate your visit to Grand Serenity Island."

This was when the crowd usually departed. But there'd been nothing normal about this tour so far, so Val should have known better than to expect that.

The woman with the Southern drawl came up first, asking for an autograph and picture from Roland. He smiled and obliged. And then repeated that task for the next seven women who did the same. Val watched as he easily slipped his arm around each woman's shoulders, leaning in so as to make each picture look personal, intimate, even. The women were glowing, their smiles big and bright—even the ones that were with their husbands—which amused Val, but probably annoyed their men. Roland also talked to each one of them, asking where they were from, how long they were staying on the island and what they liked most about Grand Serenity. The most intriguing part of that was that Val was certain he actually listened to each woman's reply.

The great womanizer was being attentive and patient, and looking damn good in the process.

And she was being silly.

With a shake of her head she moved a little closer and announced that the picture Roland had just smiled for was the last one. Of course she received irritated stares, but she didn't mind. Adults never liked being told what to do and when to do it. She knew that because she'd hated when her father had done the same. But this was different. This was work. It was her job to have this foyer clear within ten minutes of closing time. If they moved down toward the gift shop, that was fine, as it was a separate building and the exhibit halls could be locked off while the store stayed open.

"Thank you, everyone, for visiting Grand Serenity," Roland said, backing up her statement that the museum was closing.

"We hope you enjoy your time here," Val added.

She said this to every group after every tour, but this time she knew they'd enjoyed the tour. If nothing else on this island pleased them, this would have been enough.

When the last person was through the archway, Val walked to the circular desk closest to the door. It was white marble, and black letters on the wall behind it read Tour Information. That's where she worked. It was where the tours were booked and started. In a safe behind that desk were her purse and jacket. She bent down to work the combination lock and retrieve them.

"Let's get some dinner," he said the moment she stood.

"What—excuse me?" she asked, and then cleared her throat. "I mean—"

"Dinner. You know, the last meal of the day. You sit down and eat and think of all the right and wrong things you may have said or done over the last twelve hours."

He was leaning on the desk now, the darkness of his

suit in contrast to the crisp white decor. He wasn't giving her the full Reckless Royal smile, just a slight lift of his lips in the right corner. But that was enough. She reacted even as she wished she hadn't. Her cheeks warmed, just as they had earlier, and she licked her lips nervously.

"I'm sure you have better things to do, Your Highness," Val answered. Willing her fingers not to shake as she pushed her arms into her jacket, she cleared her throat and continued. "Or was there a reason you came to the museum today? I probably should have asked this before, but should I get the manager? I'm sure he's still here. I can just—"

She came around the desk and attempted to walk across the foyer once more to head toward the staff offices on the other side, but he touched her elbow again to stop her. Maybe it was just this particular spot…she'd never have guessed her elbow would be an erogenous zone…but each time he touched her there—

"I came to ask you to dinner so that we can clear the air," Roland told her, cutting off her thoughts.

Val shook her head. "There's no need," she insisted and moved her arm slowly out of his grasp.

He looked down, watching as she slipped her purse onto her shoulder. "I'm fine. You're fine. We should just go our separate ways."

Roland seemed to contemplate her words—for much longer than Val thought was necessary—before finally giving a little nod.

"I'll agree that we're both fine. But I'm hungry and after being on your feet all day, I'm sure you are, too. So let's just get something to eat and get that part of the evening out of the way."

It occurred to her to refuse again. Yes, she thought, that was the best thing to do. Her father could be a mean drunk whose debts were far larger than his bank account, and for that Val had endured her share of pitying looks and uninvited advice from the citizens of Grand Serenity. The deal her father had supposedly made for her to marry Prince Kristian was another source of contention where Val and the good people of Grand Serenity were concerned. They'd whispered about her and the prince all her life, and when the prince finally announced that there was nothing between them and that he would be marrying another woman, the whispers turned into vicious gossip. The poor little town girl trying to get into the palace.

Val didn't know which situation she despised more. What she did know was that she was sick and tired of it, and she definitely did not want to do anything to spark any more stares or whispers or gossip about herself. So she should tell Prince Roland no. She could have dinner on her own, as she had planned.

"Come on, don't be afraid," Roland told her. "I'm hungry, but I won't bite. I promise."

The expertly cut goatee went a long way to giving him a mature and masculine vibe. But it was that devilish grin, the twinkle in his rich brown eyes and the divine way in which that damn suit fit his toned and muscular frame, that were the deal breakers.

"I'm not afraid of you," was her reply. "And I'm in the mood for pasta."

Chapter 3

It rarely rained on Grand Serenity, less than twenty-five inches were received a year.

This evening, it *was* raining.

Roland could see the splatter of drops on the window as they sat in the corner booth at Jacobi Pearson's restaurant by the sea. It was an old-world place with its peeling yellow paint and the frayed faux-straw umbrellas over the tables on the outside. The inside walls were painted a muted brown, the room had cement floors and there were booth seats with splitting upholstery. It was the last place on this island that a prince should be seen having dinner, yet Roland found himself there at least once a week when he was home.

"It's the best spicy shrimp pasta I've ever had." He spoke after being lost in his thoughts for a few moments.

She hadn't seemed to mind him not talking, as she appeared engrossed in her meal and her own thoughts, as well. Originally he'd intended to watch her, something Roland had yet to figure out why he was doing in the first place. Valora Harrington was no doubt an attractive woman, but she was far from the blatantly sexy, worldly women Roland was used to passing the time with. Case in point, the last woman Roland had shared a meal with was Delayna Loray Montoya, a Brazilian heiress who hated her father but loved his money. She was gorgeous and rich and almost as reckless with her life and her finances as Roland was reputed to be. They'd spent a whirlwind weekend together in Rio where Roland could scarcely remember leaving the hotel room. Then, on Monday morning, he'd been on a jet headed to Milan where he played poker for the next two days and took an important meeting on the third. That had been three months ago. Roland hadn't seen or spoken to Delayna since then, and they were both completely fine with that fact.

Valora Harrington was homegrown. She represented everything that Grand Serenity was—at least, how Roland saw the island through his mother's eyes. Hope. Perseverance. Dignity. Those three words were printed just beneath the Grand Serenity emblem on everything a tourist could possibly purchase from the island. To Roland, they'd been ingrained in his mind. Today, he thought, was the first time he'd seen them in a person.

"It is definitely amazing," she replied as she finished another bite and took a sip from her wineglass. "Thank you, Your Highness, for suggesting this. I haven't had time to visit some of our local treasures in a while."

"You're a tour guide. Surely you recommend this place to our tourists," he commented while tearing off a piece of the crusty, still-warm bread that was served with their meal.

She had been a lot neater with her bread, breaking off a little piece and buttering it with the small knife. If he were at the palace in the formal dining room, or attending some dinner party or royal meeting, Roland would have taken more care about the crumbs, how he was sitting and who was watching. At Pearson's he was relaxed, almost as if this were the place he actually belonged, instead of some stuffy and overly formal event.

"That's all I do, is refer places on the island for visitors to see and enjoy. I'm at the museum for at least ten hours a day, six days a week. The one day I have off I usually don't spend getting around the island."

"Have you ever heard the saying, 'all work and no play'?" he asked, intrigued by what she'd just shared with him.

She tilted her head as she stared at him for a moment before replying. "You've never wondered where your next meal would come from. Never had to choose between paying the rent or the power bill."

Her lips clamped shut quickly, then she shook her head.

"I apologize. I meant no disrespect, Your Highness," she continued. "I was simply attempting to answer your inquiry."

She'd spoken the words, but she was anything but sorry, Roland thought. She was honest and there was a mole just beneath her left eye. At the edge where her eyes tilted just slightly. It was small, but dark, and he'd stared at it a bit longer than he probably should have.

"No offense taken," he replied. "You are correct. I have never wondered about those things. I understand it must have been tough with only you and your father."

She shrugged. "It is my life," was the somber reply.

"You don't sound too happy about that fact," Roland said, as he finished chewing the piece of bread he'd slipped into his mouth. It wasn't because he was still hungry, but more because he'd needed something to do with his hands. Anything to quell the urge to reach out and touch her.

She had slim fingers and wore no rings. Her nails were short but had a sheen to them, as if coated with clear polish. She wore no jewelry, he thought, except for tiny pearl earrings. Her slim neck was bare, the collar of her white polo shirt resting against skin that appeared to be warm, soft, touchable.

"I've learned that life isn't all about happiness," she replied. "Yet I believe that everyone has their own path to walk. Along that path will be things that make that person feel happy or sad, complete and fulfilled. Different scenarios strike different people in an array of ways. We handle them the best we can and continue on."

She was good at continuing on, Roland thought. He'd noticed that at the museum when the woman had brought up Valora's previous engagement to his brother. Regretting that his appearance had sparked the memory for the woman and possibly embarrassed Valora, he'd taken over and Valora had simply continued on. She'd walked with the group as if she were the tourist instead of the guide for the remainder of the tour. When she'd really wanted to get away from him and the memory as fast as she could, she'd hesitantly agreed to join him for dinner. Yes, Valora was certainly used to continuing on.

"Well," he said, picking up his napkin to wipe his hands. "Everyone deserves some happiness. I believe that's a requirement."

"It's easier said than done for some." She finished her glass of wine. "Which reminds me that I should really be going. The food and the company was a really nice gesture. Thank you again, Your Highness."

He was going to get tired real quick of the stilted way in which she addressed him. The immediate answer to that would have been to take her home, drop her off and be on his way. There was really no need for him to see or speak to Valora Harrington again.

Seeing her today had been sort of impromptu. He'd had a meeting at one of the hotels in town. From the window of the hotel he was able to see the museum. It had been a few weeks since he'd attended the opening of the new Renaissance exhibit there, and even longer since he'd walked through the hall dedicated to the royal family. It was there that one of the first portraits of his parents and their young children hung. Kris had been five and already distinguished looking in his white pants and navy blue jacket with its bright gold buttons, standing by their father's right side.

Roland wore the same outfit, but he was only three and so his jacket appeared a little big and his pants hung over his shoes as he held on to his father's leg. His mother was seated, holding a barely one-year-old Samantha, dressed in a white dress and bonnet, on her lap. That picture never failed to make Roland feel a combination of happy and sad. Homesick, he thought. Even though it was in the museum his mother had founded, on the island he'd called home all his life. He always looked at that portrait and longed for that moment in time.

So, stumbling across Valora and her group had absolutely been unplanned, but the moment he saw her he'd felt the urge to clear the air. To make sure there were no hard feelings or even bruised ones from the previous night.

"I settled things with your father," he told her, as if the thought had just popped into his head. "I also expressed my utter disappointment in the fact that he would use you as a source of repayment."

She dropped her napkin on the table and sat back against the cushioned seat.

"I feel like I've been apologizing for him all my life," she told him with a sigh. "He doesn't really mean any harm. He's just searching for a life that's not meant to be."

"His search should not embarrass you," Roland stated evenly. "He should, however, stop drinking and gambling. He's not good at either."

She gave a quick chuckle and ran one hand through the short strands of hair just above her right ear. "I've been telling him that for much longer than I care to admit."

Roland knew Valora had been her father's caretaker when it should have been the other way around. He was certain he didn't like that fact.

"Anyway, thanks again," she said and stood to leave. "Dinner was wonderful."

"Yes, it was," he told her. "And not just because of the food. I thoroughly enjoyed the company, as well."

"Oh, ah, thank you again," she replied.

He noted how shocked she looked at his words. Possibly more shocked than he was for saying them. Quiet public dinners weren't normally what he would call a nice time with a woman. Private meetings in hotel rooms or meals in secluded parts of a restaurant, from which he and his date could eventually be whisked off into the backseat of a car and driven to a hotel, were more to his liking.

"I'll take you home," he told her when he thought she might try to walk out of the restaurant as if she had her own means of transportation here.

"Thank you again, Your Highness."

She spoke politely and had even given a respectful nod of her head. Everything this woman had done so far had been cordial. There seemed to be no ill feelings toward him or even her father after the odd events of the previous night. So Roland's job was done. He could take her home and be done with the matter entirely.

The sudden urge for something more was strange and disconcerting. So he tried ignoring those thoughts.

Val was officially tired of thanking him. She knew she must sound like a complete idiot, with nothing better to say than "thank you." It was pathetic.

So, during the ride back through town, she'd opted to keep quiet. That was, until the car came to a stop in an area she knew was fifteen minutes from her house. The rain had been coming down at a pretty steady pace when they'd run to Roland's car and jumped inside. He drove a sporty little vehicle, which did not surprise her at all. The car fit his personality perfectly. Sleek and controlled with a bold hint of danger. What did not fit was that he was driving himself around instead of having a driver like the rest of the royal family. She'd noticed this last night, as well, but wasn't going to ask the prince about it.

The fact that she'd just had dinner with the prince—the Reckless Royal, at that—was not lost on her. It had been a surreal experience, one that should have had her giddy with excitement. Except she'd known it was his pity gift to her. Val hated pity, almost more than she hated the situation her father had created for them. She'd seen how the waitress looked at her when she'd brought their meal. While the woman had remained silent, Val knew very well who she was and what she was thinking.

Her name was Idelle Masoya and she lived a block over from Val. Idelle was friends with Cora Sorenza, a woman who had slept with Val's father years ago. Hugo and Cora had been an item for about six months, during which time Cora swore that Hugo stole money from her and gambled it away. She'd also accused Hugo of tearing up her house one night when he was in a drunken rage. After that night, their love affair was over.

No formal charges were filed against Hugo for destruction of property or stealing from Cora, but the damage was done. Cora spent the following years telling anyone within earshot about Hugo Harrington and his nefarious ways. By default, Cora disliked Val. She had spread it around town that Val was an enabler and just as foolhardy as her father, claiming it was the reason Prince Kristian severed ties with her. It was a sordid tale that contained more fabricated details each time it was retold. Val figured the retelling had taken place at least a thousand times in the past few months.

Val knew that at this very moment Idelle was likely in the back room of that restaurant, huddled in a corner with her cell phone to her ear, replaying to Cora everything she'd just seen—completely exaggerated. By tomorrow morning the story would have spread the couple of blocks that made up the Old Serenity neighborhood where they still lived. From there, it would only take another day or so to travel around the island.

With a sigh at the inevitable, Val turned to ask the prince, "Why are we stopping?"

"I had a question for you," he said.

They were too close, only a console and gear shift separating them in the front seat of the car. With this in mind, Val turned to the side to face him. Part of her back was now pressed against the door. She figured that was about as far away as she could to manage to get.

"Okay," she replied, even though she was thinking that he could have continued driving while he asked her a question.

"When's the last time you danced?"

"What?"

"Danced," he repeated. "When is the last time you forgot about everything around you? Every person. Every situation. Everything but the space where you could let go and simply dance?"

"I know you're not drunk because you only had one glass of wine," she said, and then quickly bit her own tongue for being so flippant with the prince.

It was just that he wasn't acting very prince-like at

the moment. His question was odd. The way he was looking at her was disconcerting. The pitter-patter of rain against the windows was rhythmic, almost romantic, if she were inclined to think along those lines. Val assured herself she definitely was not.

"No," Roland chuckled. "I am not drunk. Not from alcohol, anyway. But there's nothing wrong with being drunk or high off life. Sometimes, no matter what's going on, I have to remind myself of that fact. You only get one life, Val, you should be sure to live every minute of it."

"I do," she replied after tilting her head to stare more closely at him. "The last time I danced was at the Ambassador's Ball. With you."

The words seemed quiet in the interior of the car. Spoken slowly, as if she were afraid he wouldn't remember. Roland DeSaunters only recalled the women who had done something memorable in his life. Dancing with her so that Kristian could dance with the woman he was in love with was in no way memorable. Still, he was looking at her strangely and it was making Val uncomfortable.

He didn't seem out of his mind. Actually, Roland had always been reported to be the most down-to-earth of the royal children. He'd been photographed playing tennis with budding young athletes at a training camp he'd visited in Europe, toasting a couple who had just been married in a hotel in Scotland where he'd been staying, and at a restaurant at the theme park in the United States, sharing a breakfast table with an adorable three-year-old girl who was elated to finally meet a real-life prince. That had happened just a few months ago, which was why it was so fresh in Val's mind. She wasn't about to admit that she kept close tabs on the royal family, *all of them*. That would be like owning up to a dream she'd convinced herself was foolish and childish to have.

"Your idea of living life is by working all day at the museum and then returning home by yourself?" he asked, but he was shaking his head as if already replying to her answer. "That's not living at all."

"It's my life to do with as I please," she replied.

How many times had she recited those words to herself? Far too many to be normal.

"We should all be so lucky," was his quick retort. "I feel like dancing."

"There's no music," she quipped, and this time she looked out the window.

It had grown dark outside, the clouds helping nightfall to arrive earlier. Heavy drops came down with a steady rhythm, moving in rivulets over the car windows.

"There's always music in your heart," he answered.

His voice sounded wistful that time, and Val couldn't stop herself from turning to stare at him. He was looking out the front windshield, no doubt seeing nothing but the water raining down.

"My mother used to say that," he told her, and then smiled as he looked at her. "She loved to dance and swore she never needed a record playing to do so."

"I have no memories of my mother," Val admitted, again without being able to stop herself, or at least monitor what she was saying. "She died when I was born."

"They may be gone from this spiritual plane, but

they're always with us," Roland said as he reached a hand over to rest on hers.

For a few stilted moments Val could only stare down at their hands. His skin was a shade darker than her butter-toned complexion. He had manicured nails. There were no rings on his right hand or on her left. They were still, and yet, deep inside, Val could swear she felt something moving, shifting, changing.

"We cannot dance in the car," she said, and then cleared her throat because she thought her voice sounded rough.

"Then we'll get out," he told her, and with his free hand he pushed a button somewhere that had the door locks releasing with a loud click.

"It's raining," she announced.

"It's fine," he countered.

"No. It's not."

"What are you afraid of?" he asked. "What do you think will happen if you do something unorthodox for once in your life?"

"N-n nothing," she stammered. "I mean, I don't know. I never thought about dancing in the rain."

"That's it right there."

He gripped her fingers at that point, squeezing until she looked up at him.

"You don't think. You just do. Open the car door, step out and dance!" he told her. "I dare you to simply let go of all those thoughts and just do it."

Val didn't like to be dared. She didn't like people to think she was afraid of anything, either. Fear led to vulnerability and she never wanted to be vulnerable to anyone, ever. She was sliding her hand from his grip before her thoughts could catch up with her motions. Her other hand was on the door handle when she looked up at him.

"I'm not afraid of anything," she announced. "Especially not a dare from you."

"Prove it," he demanded, and then he smiled. The full grin in his deep brown eyes reached simultaneously into her chest to squeeze her heart, just lightly enough that her breath caught.

Val pulled on the handle and pushed the door open. She didn't think as she stepped out and felt the cool rain pelting against her face. Moving away from the car, she stretched her arms out wide and turned in a circle. Giddiness rose from the pit of her stomach and she laughed before spinning around again. The next spin was with her head held back, eyes wide-open to the drops that fell, dripping into her mouth and sliding down her face.

It was cool and refreshing and, in a sense, liberating. She didn't care who saw her, hadn't even thought of who might come along this part of the road and find her there. Her own laughter had filled her mind so she could no longer hear thoughts that might tell her she was insane or acting foolish. When the spinning had her becoming dizzy she stopped, but continued to move her feet.

With this motion Val hummed a tune she'd heard her father play late some nights. It was slow and sad—a love song, Val was certain. Still, she danced to it, moving her feet and then her hips and upper body. She danced and imagined the song was happier and that hearing it made two people feel safe and loved. It joined them and held them close together through all eternity.

Yes, she thought, it was their song. Her parents had a song and it had made them happy at one time. Val continued to move, continued to sway with the music that only she could hear.

She was so in tune with herself and her thoughts and the brimming emotions, she'd forgotten she wasn't alone. That was, until his hands slipped around her waist and she felt herself being turned around.

Val opened her eyes and looked up at him. Rain drops were heavy on her lids and she blinked quickly, still able to see him as clearly as if they were back sitting in the car. His face was as wet as hers, drops of rain falling on his lips. They weren't too thick, but just thick enough, she thought, and then wondered why she was thinking about his mouth at all.

His fingers splayed at her lower back as he gathered her closer. Their bodies were touching, wet shirt against wet shirt, so close they were now heartbeat to heartbeat. Her arms were still in the air from her dancing, and she brought them down slowly, letting her hands rest on the soaked material of his suit jacket. She heard thunder.

No, that was the incessant beat of her heart as she realized with a start that he was leaning in closer. His head was moving down, toward hers. She tilted hers back a little, not sure what to expect but wanting to be ready. Yes, she definitely wanted to be ready.

"You should do this more often," he whispered, his breath warm against her rain-chilled nose.

"Do what?" she asked, more than a little confused at the moment. Was she supposed to be following her mind or her body?

Her mind said she was chilly and getting soaked,

now that she'd stopped dancing. Her body, on the other hand said, he was keeping her warm.

"This," he said in the barest whisper, just before his lips touched hers.

She didn't say a word. Instead, Val pressed into him, tilting her head to the side to slant her lips over his. Warmth continued to spread throughout her body, even before he parted his lips just enough so that his tongue could slip out. Her lips had been wet from the rain but now they were moist from the touch of his tongue. Her lips parted, exactly what her body—and now, her mind—wanted them to do.

His hands moved farther up her back, holding her tightly as his tongue plunged deeper, exploring in a steady and persistent fashion. Val did some studying of her own. The feel of his arms around her was pleasurable. The scent of his cologne as she inhaled was dreamy. The touch of his tongue was *damn*—the only word she could come up with at the moment to describe what she felt.

At that moment a big splash of water hit her and Val instinctively pulled back from him. He was frowning and they both looked over to see that a car had just whizzed past them. It had obviously driven through a puddle and spattered the two people who were—no doubt, strangely—standing on the side of the road.

"Guess we should get going," Roland said.

"Yeah, I guess we should," Val replied quickly.

They walked back to the car without touching, but Val's thoughts remained fixated on their kiss. Even as she slipped into the passenger seat, thankful for the leather interior, she thought about the kiss and then she thought about the man.

Prince Roland Simon DeSaunters had kissed her. She'd been kissed by a prince. Deliciously.

Chapter 4

Two days later Roland stood in front of the windows that stretched the entire side of the house, rubbing a finger over his lips. He didn't know how many hours he'd spent in this very spot, thinking the same thought since he'd come in out of the rain that night.

Why had he kissed Valora Harrington?

Because she'd looked…how had she looked?

He didn't even need to close his eyes to recall, the vision was still so clear in his mind. The black pants and white shirt that made up the museum staff uniform was ordinary on everyone else who worked there. But the way the pants fit the curves of Val's hips and bottom was not ordinary at all. Extraordinary would be more like it, he thought, as he recalled seeing her walking with her guests. He didn't need to look at the top half of her body again; he'd seen that pretty clearly Friday night at her father's house, so he knew she had full breasts. He also figured those breasts would fit nicely in the palms of his hands. Actually, he thought with a twitching in his pants, they might overflow his palms.

His mouth watered at that moment. Not because he was thinking about palming her breasts or even rubbing his hand over her plump backside. This reaction was solely a result of the kiss. The memory was never far from his mind, no matter what task Roland might be doing. She'd tasted sweet, even though they'd just had the spicy pasta. Her lips had been warm, even as they'd stood outside in the chilly rain. And when she'd leaned in to him, Roland had felt the strangest thing. He'd felt needed.

Now, there was no doubt in Roland's mind that each time he'd been with a woman, that woman had needed something from him. Sex was the top need and want in *his* dealings with women because that was all Roland had ever intended to give any of them. Did Val need sex? Roland shook his head. That thought didn't sit well with him, even though it had his erection hardening almost to the point of distraction.

The doorbell ringing pulled him from his thoughts, and Roland dropped his arms to his sides and walked through the living room toward the front door. He hadn't been expecting anyone. Then again, he never expected anyone to visit him, because nobody knew about his private home except his family.

"I thought I'd find you here," Kris said the moment Roland opened the door.

"I live here," Roland replied as he stepped aside while his brother walked in.

At the end of the driveway was a white Mercedes. Roland lifted a hand to wave at Tajeo, Kris's driver. The man honked the horn in response and Roland smiled as he closed the door behind himself.

"What brings you here, brother dear?" Roland asked as he followed Kris into the living room.

Roland avoided the windows and took a seat on the ultrasoft leather couch. It was a deep burgundy color, almost like a red wine, and melded to his body each and every time he sat on it. The amount he'd paid the designer in Milan meant nothing compared to the comfort.

"You haven't been at dinner the last couple of nights, and Sam was certain you hadn't left the island, so I figured this was where you were," Kris stated solemnly.

Actually, it wasn't really solemn, it was Kris's usual tone. His older brother was a serious man. An important man, a man with the weight of the world on his shoulders. It may have only the weight of the people of Grand Serenity, but still, Roland imagined that had to feel like the whole world. He didn't really know, since he was the second born. The only way Roland would ever rule this island would be if his father and brother died. A thought he never in all his life had entertained. Not simply because he did not want to rule the island, but because he didn't know how he would live without either man in his life.

"What's going on?" he asked Kris. "You look like you've got something on your mind.

Kris unbuttoned his suit jacket and gathered his pants

slightly before taking a seat on the matching love seat across from where Roland sat.

"More like having too many *somethings* on my mind," Kris replied, and released a sigh.

His brother sat back and let his shoulders relax. They had oftentimes been as close as twins. It was like that with all three of them. As royal children, finding sincere and trustworthy friends wasn't always easy. As such, the DeSaunters siblings had opted to depend on and confide in each other.

"Wife, father, work or mom-to-be?" Roland asked with a raised brow.

"All of the above, except Malayka will never be my mother. I don't care how many rings Dad puts on her finger," Kris said, and ran his hands over his thighs.

Roland watched Kris's motions. Tension surrounded him like a dark cloud. On another man, worry might have furrowed his brow, but not Kris. His facial features were set, so that he looked just as he did in a photograph taken months ago in the paper, or even years ago in their last family photo. There was no change. Ever. There couldn't be.

As for Roland, he could clench his teeth and give a quick shake of his head at the monotony of it all. Being a prince wasn't as glamorous as he was sure some thought. How many times had he said those words? How many days had he realized that same fact over and over again?

"Do you think he's in love with her?" Roland asked Kris.

"Yes," Kris answered without hesitation. "I know he is, and so do Sam and Landry. We can all see that he loves her and that he's never loved any other woman since Mom. That's the hardest part of this situation."

"I agree," Roland said.

It was hard to accept that his father was in love with someone other than his mother. Sure, years had passed since her death, but that didn't mean Roland was ready to see another woman standing beside his father wearing that crown.

"He comes first," Kris continued. "Dad's safety, his happiness, it all comes before any feelings we have toward her or this marriage."

"I know that," Roland agreed. "Any word on Amari Taylor's escape?"

"Gary hasn't found him yet," Kris said as he clasped his fingers together. "At the jail, his cell door was simply unlocked and the guy just walked out. We're sure that means someone on the inside helped him, and since nobody confessed to being the culprit, every officer that was working the night of the escape has been fired."

Roland shook his head. "You fired all of them?"

"Yes," Kris stated. "I'm not going to play games with my family's lives. If there's no allegiance to the monarch or to justice, then they do not belong on the police force."

He heard his brother's words and, to an extent, understood them perfectly. Still, a part of Roland thought about innocent officers who may now be out of work because of this incident. On the other hand, his father could have lost his life in a car crash and Sam could have been killed when Kendon Arnold, the man they suspected of working for Amari, took shots at her. That was in addition to how many lives could have been lost during that explosion at the palace. In the end, Roland knew Kris was right, there was no more time to play or second-guess. This situation was dire.

"Sam says she misses her husband and longs for a normal life," Kris continued.

"Don't we all," Roland quipped.

"No. We don't."

His brother's response was quick and curt.

"This is my life," Kris continued. "Now, with Landry by my side, I feel like it's finally complete. Like she was meant to be there to help me through this journey. I have no doubt that I was meant to rule Grand Serenity one day and that Landry will help me with that. We'll have a family and we'll be happy here. One day."

"Wow," Roland replied with a sigh. "I wish my future was that clear."

It was the truth, he thought, as he sat back in his chair. He did wish that he knew what he wanted for his future. He wished there was a plan for him, a goal, a woman...

"Brunson said you played poker with the casino owner a few nights ago."

Kris's words were a cool statement, one filled with judgment. But Roland wasn't offended. He was used to being judged by people, even his family. They'd done so all his life.

"It was an interesting game," he replied.

Interesting seemed like a good word for what had happened that night. As for how Roland had spent the next evening, well, he was still trying to figure out how to describe that. Luckily, he didn't have to, not to Kris, anyway.

"You won," Kris said, a semblance of a smile forming. "That's my brother."

Roland grinned. "Winning is always preferred."

Kris chuckled then. "Dad said Grandpa always told him that."

"Really? Dad never mentioned that to me."

"Maybe because you don't talk to him as much as Sam and I do."

"I don't please him as much as you and Sam do," Roland quickly corrected. "But that's not what I want to talk about. Let's try going over why you have one of the guards reporting my every move to you. Am I a suspect in what's been going on now?"

"Don't be ridiculous," Kris countered. "Of course you're not a suspect. But you are a part of this mess. If they're gunning for one of us, all of us are affected. The guards are there to protect you and the rest of the family."

"Are they reporting on what Sam does? Who she sees? How long she stays out?"

"Sam isn't playing poker with people who do business within our country. And she's not at the museum telling tourists that there may be buried treasure in the castle."

So he knew that Roland had gone to the museum, as well. Roland wondered when, or if, Kris was going to ask the million-dollar question.

"Sam is living her life. She married the man of her dreams. She's continuing her work with the children here, and now in the United States, which will soon be her second home. Everything she does is rooted in who she is and what she's always wanted to become. Me, I'm doing the same thing."

Kris shook his head.

"You're stalling," Kris told him. "That's what you've always done. But one of these days, Ro, you're going to have to grow up. When you do, you'll have to decide who the adult Roland DeSaunters is going to be. A professional poker player? A womanizer? Whatever it is, you'll have to decide for yourself and stand by it. Are you ready to do that?"

"I don't have to answer that," Roland countered.

He was slowly becoming agitated. He did not like that feeling, so he stood. Moving cleared his mind. It reminded him that not only was he alive, but that he was in control. He could decide where he went, what he did, how he did it. Everything was his decision and no one else's.

Kris stood as well. "You're right, Ro. You don't have to answer to me. Or to Dad or to any one of those reporters that love to write stories about you and your frequent escapades. There's only one person you'll ever have to answer to, and that's yourself. Just make sure that when you do, you can be honest about everything you're doing. Everything you're saying or promising."

Roland stared at his brother and waited, because he knew it was coming.

"I was never engaged to marry Valora Harrington," Kris said. "We both know that. She knows that. Her father believes differently. And you kissing her on the side of the road will only confuse matters for her and for the people of Grand Serenity."

"I'm an adult and so is she," Roland instantly countered. "It's nobody's business what we do or where we do it. Nobody's!"

Kris shook his head. "You're wrong about that, Ro. Because, whether you like it or not, you're a prince. That's not just a title, it's a responsibility. Even for the Reckless Royal."

Roland turned away then because he wanted to curse. He actually wanted to throw something. But not at Kris. He knew his brother was just doing his job. As always. He had to come and say something to his younger brother. He had to correct the wrongs before they could affect the country. Roland knew that. He hated it, but he knew it.

"She's been through enough, man. Just leave her alone. We've got enough going on to keep us occupied. Don't start unnecessary rumors or make her another notch in your belt. It's not fair to her. None of this has ever been fair to her."

Roland didn't move, not even when he heard his front door open and close. He stood there staring out at his mountain, wondering how soon he could be packed and get off this island.

Chapter 5

"What's this?"

"It's a picnic basket," he replied.

"I mean, what's it for?"

He tilted his head and grinned. "To have a picnic. And if you're going to ask what a picnic is, I'll save you the trouble. It's when you put a blanket on the ground, sit down and eat. Usually requires nice weather, which we have on this balmy Tuesday."

She opened her mouth to speak, but Roland continued.

"You probably want to know what's in the basket. Well, I believe Chef Murray said something about spicy tuna, lime onion rings and a crabmeat salad with her very special creamy ginger dressing. And I must admit I requested my favorite dessert of all time, rice pudding. You'll love it! She puts fresh cinnamon sticks into each cup."

The last was said as he tapped the large brown wicker basket taking up most of his backseat. Val had finished work a little earlier today than usual. She'd come out of the museum and had been heading down the street to where she'd parked her car when she saw Roland looking like a model out of a magazine as he casually leaned against that flashy sports car.

He wore beige linen slacks with a matching short-sleeved shirt. His skin looked golden or sun kissed or whatever that delectable shade was called. The leather tie-ups he wore were only a shade or so darker than his clothes, his ankles crossed as he leaned against the sleek silver car. His goatee was close and neatly trimmed along his strong jaw. The silver watch he wore sparkled in the sunlight. If she could have—and if she were still a teenager—Val might have snapped his picture with her phone and used it as her screen saver.

The thought made her dizzy and disgusted at the same time. She was not drooling over this guy. Of all the men in the world, not this one.

It was almost six in the evening, and while the sun was still shining, it would be setting soon. People still moved about the street. Tourists headed to some of the souvenir shops up and down the corridor, and some waited at the trolley stop on the corner. Cars drove down the cobblestone path, some slowing to look at Prince Roland's car. One even stopped and a man hung out his window to take a picture.

It was at that moment that Val realized Roland was

waiting for her to respond as she stood there staring around like some lost schoolgirl.

"I have a pot of soup at home," she blurted out.

He grinned. "So you'd rather have soup than tuna and rice pudding?" Before she could answer, he shook his head. "Even if you say so, I won't believe it."

Val didn't believe herself either, so she didn't bother to say it. "You don't have to do this. I told my father not to spread any rumors about us and he agreed that it would be foolish. So we're okay, there's no need for you to feel like you have to make sure he's not going to go to the press or make any other false claims against you or the royal family."

Roland pushed away from the car and moved until he stood directly in front of her. Val, standing at five feet nine inches, tilted her head back slightly to look into his eyes. They were nice deep-brown eyes with thick lashes and eyebrows, but she insisted to herself she wasn't paying attention to any of that.

"I could have sworn I explained this to you the other night, but I'll say it again, just so we're officially on the same page," he began. "Your father and I have already spoken. That poker game, him losing to me and how we plan to work that out, is between me and Hugo. You have nothing to do with any of that."

"He's my father," she insisted.

Roland shook his head again. "We have no control over that. It just is. And the food that I had to do a lot of maneuvering to get into the backseat of this car will go to waste if you do not climb in and have this picnic with me."

"You could eat the food yourself or donate it to the children's mission," she countered.

"I could," he agreed. "Or I can have a lovely evening meal with a nice woman who I'm sure isn't just trying to get her picture taken with me."

He raised his brows while looking back at her, as if he were asking, "Got any other excuses?" Of course, those words never fell from his lips—medium-thick lips that she recalled kissing all too well.

"The last time we shared a meal together it rained," she replied.

"I already checked the forecast. Tonight will be clear," he said. Then, before she could think of another response, Roland grabbed her hand.

He tugged her gently toward the car before saying, "Come on, it's just a blanket and food. Nothing more. Nothing less. What's the worst that could happen?"

This wasn't the worst circumstance, Val thought. In fact, it was the best picnic she'd ever been invited to, and she had yet to taste any of the food.

She should have known it wouldn't just be a blanket and food. He was royalty, after all. Still, the effort and thought that she presumed had gone into this setup was reason enough for her to relax and enjoy.

There was a wood canopy—like maybe some of the palace staff had been out there all day building the dwelling just for them. Sheer white curtains hung along three sides, blowing slowly in the breeze. Through the open fourth side she could see a fluffy white blanket had been spread over the sandy ground area. On that blanket, six large white pillows were lined up along the back. On one side was a huge silver ice bucket with two bottles sticking out of it. Wicker serving trays held martini glasses that had already been filled with strawberries and blueberries. In the center was a crystal bowl containing more fruit, and arranged in a lovely tropical design. This all meant there had to definitely be someone else there besides them. She looked around, but did not see anyone. They were most likely paid well to be discreet—out of sight and out of mind. She sighed and looked into the distance toward the crystalline water that rolled onto the sandy shore while the bluest sky provided a perfect backdrop.

"Have a seat," he said as he came up behind her and moved around so that he could set the basket on the blanket.

The white looked so pristine, the scene so serene and perfect and…romantic. She hesitated, but only for a moment. Even though doubts swirled in her mind, the last thing she wanted the prince to think was that she was indecisive or immature. Val took a step and then looked down at the black boat shoes she always wore to work. Hurriedly toeing them off, she stepped first one and then the other bare foot onto the softest cotton she thought she'd ever felt in her life.

When she finally sat, it was with her back to the pillows and the water. She crossed her legs beneath her and watched as Roland also removed his shoes and moved across the blanket. He sat beside her, pulling the basket close enough so that he could reach into it without getting up.

"Here are two glasses. You can pour whichever wine you prefer and I'll fix our plates," he said.

Roland handed her the glasses without even checking to see if she planned to do as he asked. He was used to that, she surmised. People just jumped to do what the prince wanted. Women would do somersaults to impress him, to be sitting beside him on this beautiful day about to share a meal. Val knew that all too well. She knew precisely what it was like to dream of this moment with a prince, or rather, with her very own knight in shining armor.

Only this wasn't the man she'd dreamed of, or at least, she didn't believe it was. The man in her dreams, the one who came and swept her away from everything that had ever caused her pain or strife, had always been faceless in her slumber. To Val, that made the dream so much more romantic and possibly attainable. But, today, she thought the dream might have been nicer if the face she saw just before she awakened was Roland's.

Clearing her throat and hopefully her delusional thoughts, Val did as Roland had instructed. She selected the white wine that she knew was from the vineyards owned by a member of Princess Vivienne's family in the United States. As a show of support, every restaurant and bar on Grand Serenity served this brand. It was a little expensive, so Val only consumed it on special occasions. Her father refused to drink it at all.

"This is yours," he said, handing her a real china plate of food. "Wasn't sure how much you wanted, but we have plenty if you want seconds."

Roland continued to fix his own plate, one filled with a good deal more food than he'd put on hers, and then he settled back to lift his glass. Turning to her, he said, "Let's toast to picnics and sea air."

He looked fantastic sitting there with a glass in one hand, his plate in the other, the sheer curtain billowing behind him and the rolling sea in the distance beyond. He could be on a postcard inviting all to visit Grand Serenity Island. If he were, Val figured tourism would increase by no less than eighty percent. That is, if someone actually ran with the postcard idea. She, for one, knew she'd visit if this guy were inviting her to a Caribbean island.

With a slight shake of her head, she lifted her glass and moved it until it clinked lightly with his. "To picnics, sea air and strange days."

"Strange days, indeed," Roland said quietly after he sipped from his glass and set it on one of the serving trays in front of them.

It occurred to her then that maybe this picnic wasn't about her or her father at all. Roland had already begun eating, so Val joined in. What she did not do was say anything to him. Even though there were several questions rolling through her mind at the moment.

"This crab salad is wonderful," she remarked minutes later, when the silence begin to border on frustration.

"Ms. Murray's been cooking for our family for as long as I can remember," he said, having long finished the heaping portion of salad he'd put on his own plate. "I guess she must have been in her teens when I was a youngster because she only looks to be about twenty-nine today."

Val smiled. "I'm sure she loves hearing you say that."

He shrugged. "I can't help if it's the truth."

Val was sure that Ms. Murray would believe any

compliment coming from Roland, with his charismatic smile and undeniable charm, as the truth. Any woman would believe anything he said, whenever he said it. She wondered how it felt to have that type of power.

"You want to hear something else that's the truth?" she asked, without considering whether or not she should.

Roland immediately turned to look at her. "Yes, that would be refreshing."

"Why?" she asked yet another question, but this time she answered it herself. "Because you're not used to women telling you the truth. Or rather, you're inclined to always believe what they say is a lie."

He waited a beat, his gaze never wavering before he replied. "It comes with the territory. The resistance to trust, I mean. Like it or not, I'm a hot commodity. Cautiousness was taught to me at a very young age." He'd smiled as if he were joking, but she could tell he totally believed in what he had said.

"I've learned to be cautious, as well," she replied, not at all offended by his comments about being a hot commodity.

To someone else those words may have sounded arrogant or possibly conceited. To her, ironically, they were honest. Roland was being honest with her, even though he didn't trust any woman to give him the same in return.

"You never know what people truly think about you when all they've ever heard was gossip," she admitted.

"Misjudgments," Roland commented, as his eyes seemed to search her face for something she wasn't quite sure she possessed. "People tend to do that far too often."

"I agree," she said, her throat suddenly dry.

"Honesty is a beautiful thing," he continued as he rubbed his hands down his thighs.

"It can be," Val replied. "On the other hand, some people can't accept the truth as well as they can a lie."

"You want to know what's true at this very moment?" Roland asked.

Was he leaning closer?

Val clenched the napkin she'd been holding tightly in her hand.

"What?" she asked in response.

She didn't really think she wanted to know what Roland was going to say next, but at the same time, she didn't want this moment to end.

He was leaning closer, so that now he'd planted a palm on the blanket to hold himself steady as his face neared hers.

"I want you," he whispered.

She gulped, loudly. Then she licked her lips impulsively as she watched his gaze lower to her mouth.

"Yes, Valora, I definitely, unquestionably want you."

Val did not respond. Or rather, she did, similarly to the way she had the last time his lips touched hers. She kissed him back. This time with fervor that came from out of nowhere, whisking down over them and crashing into her chest as she opened her mouth to his.

He'd said it and, yes, Roland meant it. More than he feared he'd ever meant anything in his life. He wanted this woman.

While wanting a woman was nothing new to Roland, this was different. He wanted Valora on a totally different level than he had ever desired anyone else. Was that strange? Yes. He'd decided that about ten seconds after he'd called to reserve the jet. After Kris's impromptu visit, Roland had been ready to leave Grand Serenity for one of his little vacations.

Now, he was glad he'd stayed.

She tasted like honey. Even after the spicy seafood and fruit, she still tasted sweet. And warm. Her tongue stroked slowly against his and Roland's body heated all over. His fingers itched to touch her. His growing erection throbbed and Roland knew in that instant that he was in big trouble.

She pulled away before he could think of what to do next. Continuing their kiss and seeing where it led was currently high on his list of priorities.

"What are you doing, Roland?" she asked him as she smoothed her hands over her hair.

He liked her hair. It was short, combed in a feathery style on top and cut even lower on the sides. The color of it was black and stark against her butter-toned skin.

"Wow, if I have to explain, I guess I'm not doing it very well," he joked, hoping to ease the sudden tension building between them.

"No," she said with a shake of her head and a tentative smile. "What are you doing here? With me?"

"I'm doing something I've never done before," he admitted.

"Why?"

She was staring intently at him, genuinely search-

ing for the answer. Roland figured he might as well
give it to her.

"Of all the people I know in this world, the ones I
love and that love me, and even the ones I've never met,
you're the only one that looks at me without judgment.
I know this because you never call me the Reckless
Royal. You don't mention the gambling or the rumors
about the women I'm supposedly involved with, and you
seem as comfortable sitting here with me as you were
walking through that museum. I like all of those things."

She licked her lips again and folded her hands in
her lap. She did not look away from him. Other women
blushed and looked down whenever he offered them a
compliment. They giggled at his jokes and acted breathless after his kisses. They fell into his bed as easily as
he slipped on a pair of pants. And, in the end, they had
absolutely no idea who he really was.

"It would have been rude to bring up any of those
things," she finally replied. "And besides, I can hardly
judge anyone considering all the stories flying around
the island about me and my father."

"Did you like being here today?" he asked.

She nodded immediately. "I did. But it can't happen again."

"Why? You don't want to eat really good food and
sit on the beach again?"

Her head shook slightly. "I don't want the next rumor
to be that I've gone from your brother to you," she replied.

The words had come quick and succinctly, as if she
were making a definitive statement that he shouldn't

even consider debating. Unfortunately for her, Roland never did anything that was expected of him.

"For the first time in my life I can be near a woman and not see dollar signs in her eyes or hear the feigned adoration in her tone. I can breathe easily and speak freely. I know, because you've already had your own run-ins with gossip and whispers behind your back, that you respect my privacy."

"There's no such thing as privacy on this island, Your Highness."

"Stop calling me that!" he shouted and instantly regretted it.

She hadn't moved, but her expression had changed. No longer was she casually staring at him; surprise now registered across her face.

He sighed. "I mean, you can call me Roland when we're together. It's just us, so you can just say my name."

"Thank you for today, Roland," she said lightly. "It was the best picnic I've ever been on."

Roland shook his head. He was the one to turn away this time, staring out to the water as he spoke. "I'm glad to hear that. Next time I'll come up with something better."

"This was the best because it was the first," she whispered.

At the hint of sadness in her voice, Roland turned to look at her. She was staring down at an empty wineglass now, tracing a finger over its crystal rim. Her tone perfectly depicted the way he felt. Unhappy, despondent and resigned to fate. He wondered how long they would both continue with this inner struggle, unable or unwilling to do what was necessary to break free.

His phone rang, the Star Wars-themed ringtone casting a hint of humor over the otherwise somber mood.

"Episodes 4 through 6," she said as he reached into his pocket to retrieve his phone.

With the device now ringing in the palm of his hand, Roland replied with a smile, "Of course, they're the best."

She was smiling at him. A genuine smile that reflected a soft light in her eyes. Then he finally pushed the answer button on the phone and put it to his ear.

"This is Roland," he answered.

After releasing a series of curse words he said, "I'll be right there."

He disconnected the call and let his head fall back, his eyes closed.

"What's wrong? What happened?" Valora asked, but he couldn't speak.

He did not want to repeat the words he'd just heard, did not want to believe this was happening.

"Roland? How can I help?"

"It's my father," he said and started to move. "I have to go."

He was up and coming from under the canopy in seconds, signaling to the guard he knew was only about fifteen feet away.

"Command sent us a message. We're ready to go, Your Highness," Brunson told him. "You can ride in the truck with us and we'll have someone take your car back to your house."

"No," Roland replied instantly. He'd just pushed his feet into his shoes. "I can drive myself."

"I don't think that's a good idea, Your Highness. It will be safer if—"

Roland quickly cut the guard off. "It will be safer if you let me do what I want to do. Now stay here and make sure the crew gets all of this cleaned up. They're in that white truck down the road. Tell the security team I'm on my way to the hospital."

"Your Highness, I don't think you should drive yourself. I'm sure your emotions are running high and—" Brunson tried once more.

"I've got it!" Roland yelled and pulled his car keys out of his front pants pocket.

In a quick and unexpected motion the keys were snatched from his hand.

"I've got it," Valora said. "I'll drive him to the hospital."

She'd put on her shoes and was already walking in the direction of his parked car, where two other guards had been standing watch over the vehicle.

Brunson looked like he wanted to object again, but Roland's look must have warned the man against it. After all, Roland was still pissed that the guy was basically Kris's personal spy. Turning away from him, Roland felt like he should say something to Valora. But she looked determined and kind of sexy as she walked purposefully to his car and slipped behind the wheel. Besides, his father had just had a heart attack; there was no time to argue or ogle or anything else. Roland only hoped there was time to save the prince.

Chapter 6

Sisters of Serenity was the only hospital on the island, and it was located on the southern tip. The Children's Hospital had once been a smaller ward of the facility, but eventually morphed into a connecting building where only children were treated.

Roland moved swiftly through the empty halls. He was aware of the three guards that had traveled in separate cars, following him and Valora. Hospital security had been waiting at a back door when the first guard vehicle had pulled up. Roland had jumped out the moment Valora parked his car behind the guard's. Now they were boarding an elevator. Probably the service one so that he would be afforded privacy.

At this point, Roland really didn't care who saw him or what they said. All that mattered was his father.

Ellen, Dr. Beaumont's nurse had been the one to call Roland. Dr. Beaumont had been the palace doctor since Roland was born. Ellen's words had been simple and chilling.

"Your father had a heart attack. He's being rushed to Sisters now."

That was all.

But that was enough.

When the elevator doors opened, Roland rushed off with no idea of where he was going. He heard voices but did not stop walking until he felt a hand on his arm.

"We need to go this way, Your Highness."

Valora had spoken to him quietly while looking directly at him.

"Your father is down here."

She was guiding him down the hall before Roland could think of what to say. Words were jumbled in his mind at this point. Memories flashed before his eyes like a movie in fast-forward. His father had taught him how to ride a bike. The front driveway of the palace was where he'd climbed on that silver bike and ridden with the assistance of training wheels. Rafe had given him a quick command.

"Balance yourself and pedal," was all his father had said, and Roland was expected to perform.

That's how it was with Rafe. He gave an instruction and his children—namely, his sons—were expected to execute it perfectly. There was really no room for any other option.

We love you to pieces.

That had come from his mother about a month before her death. Roland had received a bad report from one of his teachers in the starchy private school he'd been sent to. His father had expressed immediate embarrassment and displeasure, while his mother had tried to quietly encourage Roland to do better. When he'd simply stared up at both of them, his mother had been the first to break, going to her knees to hug him. Over his mother's shoulder he could see his father staring down at him. Rafe did not join in Vivienne's declaration to their son, but he had nodded and winked. Roland had smiled then, and he'd relaxed. For the first time in his life his father had shown some sort of emotion toward him. He'd been elated.

Of course, that memory had had to last Roland up to this point, because there'd never been another occasion for Rafe to *wink* at his son. There'd been no occasions for the prince to even commend his son on a job well done, because Roland hadn't done a thing to please his father since. A part of him knew that it was on purpose, another part wanted to ignore all those tangled reasons and just live his life. So he slept with women, left them and gambled. Both pastimes providing just the right amount of distance for him.

Now, as he approached a door with a sign that said Waiting Area, he felt nothing but regret.

"There you are," Sam said a second after throwing her arms around his neck and hugging him close. "I was so afraid you'd gone off somewhere and wouldn't make it back here in time."

Roland hugged his sister, giving an extra squeeze, to which she immediately responded.

"I'm so afraid," she whispered.

"Don't be. He's stronger than all of us, you know

that," Roland said, even though those words weren't ringing true for him at the moment.

"What happened?" he asked when Sam finally released him.

His sister took his hand then, leading him to one of the uncomfortable-looking chairs. Gary, Sam's husband and the ex-army captain Kris had hired to overhaul and supervise the palace's new security system, sat a couple of seats away. Across the room, Kris stood with Landry right beside him. Near the door were two guards. In every corner of the room was another guard. They were everywhere all the time now, and yet his father was still somewhere in this building, possibly dying.

"We were having dinner and he just stopped talking." Malayka spoke up.

Roland turned around to see that she was sitting close to the window, her legs crossed, trembling fingers near her lips as she shook her head. Her nails were bright red, the ring his father had given her shining in the fluorescent lighting of the room. He didn't have to wonder why he hadn't noticed her before now. It was because he didn't think of her as family.

"I tried to help him but I didn't know what to do," she continued. "His face looked so ashen, then he fell out of the chair. Oh, it was horrible."

She buried her face in her hands after she'd finished speaking, and Roland turned slowly from her to look at his sister again.

"What happened?" he asked, as if he hadn't heard a word that Malayka said.

"Gary met me at the tourism board meeting after his plane landed. We knew we were running late for dinner and planned to just have something sent to our room. But I wanted to stop in the dining room to speak to Dad to let him know about the board's forecast for next year. This was just in case I didn't get a chance to see him before I left for all-day meetings scheduled for tomorrow. He was already on the floor when we came in," Sam told him.

"His pulse was faint." Gary picked up with the story. "Sam called for Dr. Beaumont. I called for an ambulance. He's in the back now."

"Dr. Beaumont says it may have been a heart attack," Kris spoke then, his gaze intent on Roland.

"He's always been healthy," Roland commented, still unable to believe they were actually at the hospital and all wondering what was going to happen to his father.

"Stress," Val said softly. "It's a silent ki… I mean, people often disregard how serious stress can be when it's not managed properly. I have to imagine that being the prince of an island is a very stressful job."

All eyes immediately went to her. All except for Roland's. He knew she was there. He'd felt her standing near him but not speaking, almost as if her presence were enough. He wondered if it was.

In the next moment the door opened and Dr. Beaumont came in. He immediately went to Kris. Gary and Sam quickly moved closer. Malayka was up and moving in before Roland could take a step. She grabbed the doctor's arm.

"What is it? How is he? When can I see him?" she asked rapidly. "He needs to know that I'm here. No, wait," Malayka added abruptly. "We shouldn't speak of the prince while outsiders are in the room."

Everyone turned then, looking in Roland's direction, but not at him. They were looking at Valora, he knew, and he didn't like it.

"I'll go," he heard her announce.

"No," he said, moving quickly to take her hand before she could turn and leave. "She will stay and you can speak freely, Dr. Beaumont. Tell us what happened to my father."

He was very aware of Kris's cool gaze in his direction, but Roland ignored it. Instead, he focused on the doctor and on how comforting Valora's hand felt in his own. While Kris stood with his wife and Sam with her husband, Roland had been acutely aware of the fact that he was standing alone. Not so much of a physical distance from his family, but still alone. The way he always seemed to feel when he was with them. With Valora by his side, some of the pain of feeling like an outsider dissipated.

Dr. Beaumont looked discreetly to Kris, waiting for the crown prince to nod his approval before continuing. Valora squeezed his hand at that moment, and when Roland looked back at her, he knew she was telling him that it was okay. In his father's absence, Kris was the head of the royal family. That had always been a fact. Today may have been the only time it irritated Roland.

"As I feared when we left the palace, the prince has suffered a heart attack," Dr. Beaumont began.

Malayka gasped and her fingers once again came to her face, trembling as she batted her eyes wildly. Sam leaned closer into Gary, and Landry put an arm around Kris's waist, as if to keep him steady.

"Is he alright now?" Sam asked, her voice clear and even, although her eyes had already filled with tears.

"He's stable," the doctor continued. "There's a blockage in one of the arteries leading to his heart. I've called for the cardiologist. The moment he arrives, we'll perform an angioplasty."

"A what?" Malayka asked, shaking her head as if she just did not understand what was going on.

"It's a stent," Landry spoke up. "It will help to open the clogged artery."

Landry was a stylist, so it wasn't abnormal for Roland and the others to look at her in wonder for knowing about this medical condition.

Dr. Beaumont gave her a nod of approval and continued to speak. "The procedure will take about an hour. We'll give him a local anesthetic and have him sedated while we work. Afterward, I expect recovery to be swift, but I would prefer he stay here at the hospital for a few days so that he can be closely monitored."

"He can be monitored at the palace," Malayka immediately announced. "He's the prince. He should not stay here among the commoners."

"He will stay where he gets the best care," Roland interjected.

"Yes, Your Highness," Dr. Beaumont said to Roland. "That is precisely what I am thinking. While I run a state-of-the-art facility back at the palace, there is no operating room or proper testing equipment there. If, which I am not anticipating, your father's condition should suddenly deteriorate, I feel much more comfortable with him receiving quick and adequate care here at the hospital."

"Then this is where he will stay," Kris stated in his official tone. "When can we see him?"

"Not until after the procedure. I want to keep him calm until we have the stent in place and he's receiving proper medication."

Malayka's arms fell to her sides, her fists balled as she stomped one sky-high-heeled foot to the floor.

"That's nonsense. I'm his wife. I demand to see him now," she said.

"You're not his wife yet," Sam said quietly.

A chill settled over the already tense room until Kris moved to stand beside Malayka. He looked regal with his shoulders squared and chin raised. Nobody was going to say another word until he spoke, not even the doctor.

"Do what is necessary to get my father back on his feet," Kris told Dr. Beaumont. "We'll wait out here until you give the okay. At that time, if you feel my father is up to it, we will visit with him briefly and then we will return to the palace to allow you and your team to do your job. The prince and his health are of the highest priority. No other issues will hinder you from taking care of him."

The look on Malayka's face said she was not happy with Kris's statement. But the way Kris had positioned himself between Malayka and the doctor said he didn't give a damn.

With a nod, Dr. Beaumont left the room. Gary immediately hugged Sam close to him as she whimpered quietly. Landry looked to Roland briefly, but then went to her husband.

"Let's sit over here, Kris," she said to him, but he was already shaking his head.

Kris turned to Malayka. "I can call for your maid to assist you while we wait," he told her. "But you will wait here, in this room, and you will remain civil. This is emotional for all of us. The less dramatics we have, the better."

"Dramatics," she hissed. "Who are you calling dramatic? I have a right to see him, regardless of who was born first."

"And you will see him," Kris replied. "But only when the doctor says it is safe. If you love him the way you proclaim, you should want only what's best for him."

Malayka looked as if she would burst with unspoken words and rage, but she wisely did not push Kris any further on this subject. Instead, she turned and stalked across the room, dropping down heavily into the seat near the window where she'd been before.

Roland watched Kris closely, so he saw the moment his brother gave the slightest nod of his head.

"I'll be right back." Roland turned to Valora. "Stay right here."

When she nodded her agreement, Roland once again felt a comfort he'd never experienced before. He didn't have time to examine it, so he simply released her hand and walked over to where Kris and Gary were now standing. Landry had put an arm around Sam and the two women took the seats farthest from where Malayka sat.

"When did she return?" Kris asked Gary about Malayka.

"Two hours before they sat down to have dinner at

six forty-five," Gary answered immediately. "The chef said the prince asked for dinner to be held until Malayka was ready."

Kris nodded. "Have you already secured the manifest from the jet?"

"Yes," Gary answered. "She left here last Monday and they flew nonstop to Chicago, Illinois."

"Malayka went back to the States?" Roland asked. "Why? Did she have some appearance there?"

"None that we know of," Kris replied. "I received a call from Siegmond late last Sunday night. He said Malayka had called him requesting the jet be ready for her first thing the next morning. Until the wedding takes place, he needs approval from one of us to move that jet. There was nothing on the schedule, but by the time I could get to Dad in his room the next morning, she was already packed and heading out."

Roland frowned. "Dad approved the trip?"

"He did," Kris answered. "And he did not give me any details as to why she had to make this impromptu trip."

"What the hell is going on with him? Why is he so blindly trusting her?" Roland asked, his frustration with his father's impending nuptials getting to him at the moment.

"He's in love," Gary stated simply. "I know what you're going to say. I thought it, at first, myself. But I've watched the two of them from a different angle. While I've grown to respect and care for Prince Rafe, I have a more objective eye than the rest of you. That's part of the reason you brought me here, Kris."

Kris nodded, even though Roland was sure his

brother was feeling the same frustration with their father and Malayka that he was.

"He loves her and I believe she loves him," Gary continued.

"She's a liar," Roland insisted.

Gary shrugged. "That's undeniable. We're still combing through her past. What I can say is that there's no college degree and no record of her cheerleading for any professional squad. What she told you and your father was a carefully constructed facade."

"Complete with a fake background that required a United States security clearance to break through," Kris added with a frown.

Gary nodded. "Yes. I had to use connections I had at the National Security Agency to get any real information on her."

"Then she is involved in the incidents that have taken place," Roland stated, the words settling with distaste in his mouth.

"I don't have undeniable proof of that just yet, and what I found for the years she told you she was in school and cheerleading was nil. She did live in Paris for a couple of years, and then she returned to the States. To Chicago, to be exact."

"So, there's someone there that knows her. Family, maybe," Kris added.

"I believe so. As soon as I make sure Sam is alright, I'm going to make a few calls. I'll find out everywhere she went during her visit in Chicago and everyone she saw," Gary told them.

"Why don't we just have somebody follow her and

report back to us daily?" Roland asked. "You know, like one of her guards."

If Kris picked up on his sarcasm, he expertly ignored it.

"Because we're not ready for any of our staff to know we suspect her yet. Besides that, we have no idea who she or Amari already had working for them," Kris answered.

"He's right. It's better that all our surveillance of her comes from outside contractors. People that neither she nor Amari would know that we've reached out to," Gary added.

Kris nodded slowly. "In the meantime, we continue as if nothing has changed," he stated. "Not with her and not with the royal family. I don't want any word of Dad's condition in the press."

The last was directed to Roland. It took him only a moment to realize why his brother was saying that to him.

"She's not the press and you know it," he stated, being careful to keep his voice lowered.

"I know she's not the press, Roland. What I'm wondering is why she's here in the first place," Kris said.

If she were his wife, there would be no question. If she were his girlfriend, there would be questions and possibly disbelief. There would be a little scandal because of her father's rumors. She'd hinted at that just a while ago when they were sitting on the beach. But Valora was none of those things. Roland could say that for sure. What he couldn't say was what she really meant to him. Why had he agreed to let her drive him here? Why had he insisted that she stay?

"She's with me," he told his brother and brother-in-law. "You know her and her family. They've lived here all their lives."

"Her father's a raving lunatic," Kris countered.

Roland couldn't argue that fact. "She's not her father, any more than I am mine. The moment I know that Dad is on the mend, I'll take her home. Until then, we'll be sitting over there and you needn't worry about anything that happens in this room being repeated by her."

He moved away before Kris or Gary could say anything more. He didn't want to hear their comments and he didn't want to answer the questioning looks they undoubtedly now had. He just wanted to sit down before his legs completely gave out on him. Before the weight of Dr. Beaumont's words about his father needing some type of heart procedure to remain alive could take full effect.

It was after midnight when Roland and Valora walked out of the hospital and climbed into his car.

He was behind the wheel this time and she fastened herself into the passenger seat. They rode in silence on the way to her house. She was certain he was thinking about his father. The prince was going to recover, the doctor had said so once the angioplasty was completed.

Valora had breathed a sigh of relief while she sat in the waiting room beside Roland. After the doctor's words he'd leaned forward with his elbows resting on his knees and dropped his head. She'd wanted to hug him in that moment, to share the relief with him in some way. From the time they'd walked into that waiting room, Roland had been tense and angry. The fear she'd seen in his eyes when he'd first received the phone call about his father had been buried. She suspected that's what he'd always done, hidden the feelings he wanted no one to see. It seemed all too similar to how she dealt with her own life. That was the reason she'd stayed when he asked her to. Or, at least, that was what Valora had told herself.

Nobody had wanted her in that waiting room tonight, and if she were completely honest with herself, she didn't blame them. Her father had been a thorn in Prince Kristian's side since he had been born. The day that Kristian had come to her house to speak with her, five months ago, she'd actually thought he was going to ask her to leave the island.

The white car had pulled slowly into the dirt driveway in front of the small house she rented in Old Serenity. The luxury vehicle looked instantly out of place beside the overgrown hedge by the passenger side of the car and the dismal garden that greeted the prince when he stepped out. As for her little house, well, it had been freshly painted at the beginning of the year, so its white exterior with blue windowsills sparkled. She'd opened the bold blue door with its tropical-themed wreath slowly, before he could even knock.

"May I come in?" he'd asked.

Valora remembered trembling as his deep voice seemed to boom around the quiet area. She'd stood as straight as she possibly could before dropping into a curtsy and bowing her head slightly. "Yes, Your Highness."

Stepping to the side, she let him into her house and closed the door behind him. He stood in the center of her living room. His broad-shouldered stance seemed much larger than the small space of the room.

"I wanted to inform you that a statement will be coming from the palace this week. It will officially deny any wedding agreement between the two of us."

He'd spoken very succinctly and slowly, as if he wanted to make sure not only that she understood, but that he was also prepared for any reaction she might have. But she'd had no reaction, except for the shock she was still grappling with at seeing the crown prince in her house to begin with. As for his words, well, she'd always known there would be no marriage between herself and Kristian DeSaunters. Not only because the agreement her father had talked about forever was a lie, but because there had never—even in the nights when a starry-eyed girl had wished upon the stars—been a moment when she'd felt anything remotely romantic toward the man.

He was handsome, there was no doubt about that. Powerful by birthright and compassionate, she figured, by choice. But he was not the man she dreamed of. Even though she had never seen that man's face, she knew instinctively he was not Kristian. Even then, as he'd stood just a few feet away from her, Val had known that he was not meant for her and she was not meant for him.

"You didn't have to come all the way down here to tell me that, Your Highness. I've known all my life that the marriage agreement was a lie. I only hate that I was unsuccessful in getting my father to admit that fact," she'd said in a tone much more relaxed than she'd imagined she could pull off.

"That is a pity. However, I feel it is time to finally put it to rest," he'd stated.

Because he'd finally fallen in love. She'd seen pictures of the prince in the local paper with an American woman. The photos were from the day they'd been at the museum for the last exhibit opening. Val had seen them in person that day, too. She'd noted that, while the woman had stayed a reasonable distance from the prince, and there had been no stolen glances or touching of any kind between the two of them, love was in the air. The connection they shared was apparent. Now, it was confirmed.

"I agree," she said quietly.

"I wish you well in your life and apologize ahead of time for any embarrassment or backlash you may experience as a result of the announcement."

"I apologize to you, Your Highness, for all that my father has done and said about the royal family. I wish it had never happened," she admitted.

"As do I," he told her before leaving.

The next time Val had seen Prince Kristian was at the Ambassador's Ball, where he had been interrupting Roland's dance with the now-princess Landry.

That was the first time she'd danced with Roland.

"It's late," Roland said, pulling her from her recollections. "I'll walk you inside."

Val hadn't realized that they'd pulled up in front of her house and that the car was now parked. Roland held the keys in his hand as he stared out the front windshield.

Val took a deep breath and released it slowly. "It's

not much," she said. "But it's private and it's mine for every thirty days that I make the rent payment."

She didn't know why she was saying all this, why she felt the need to explain where she lived and why. It was clear to both of them that this was no palace.

"Give me your keys," he said, as if he hadn't heard a word she'd said. "I'll let you inside."

Years of independence had the words, "No thanks, I can let myself in," pushing to be said. But now was not the time for taking that stance.

Roland was hurting, that was plain to see. If opening the door and letting her into her house would make him feel better, or at least give him some solace, she would let him have it. Reaching into her purse she pulled out her keys and handed them to him. Roland accepted the keys and got out of the car. By the time he made it around to her door, Val had already opened it. He held out a hand for her and she accepted before climbing out. Roland closed the car door and walked with her hand in his to the front of her house. He used the key to unlock the door and stepped inside before her.

"There's a light switch on the wall to your right," she told him.

In seconds light illuminated the living room and Val stepped inside behind him. He set her keys on the small table near the door.

"This wasn't how I anticipated this evening ending," he told her as he moved closer to the door again.

"It was an unfortunate turn of events," she said. "But he's going to recover, Roland. He's going to be just fine."

It was only the second time she'd said his name, and

Val had to admit it still felt a little odd. The way he looked at her when she'd said it, however, was something different. There was sadness in his dark brown eyes and the barest slump of his shoulders, even though he stood tall with his legs slightly parted, his hands clasped in front of him.

"He's the rock of this family," Roland stated. "He will recover."

Val nodded. He needed to say those words aloud, to remind himself.

"It's late. I'll let you go," he continued.

He had turned, his hand on the doorknob, when Val said, "Stay."

Roland stilled. Then, after a second or so, he turned his head to look at her. "What did you say?"

Val didn't know why she'd said it, all she knew was that it needed to be said.

"You shouldn't be alone tonight. Stay here with me."

He looked as if he might say no, as if there were a million and one reasons why he should go. She knew them all and had no doubt she would replay them for herself first thing tomorrow morning. But for now, for this moment in time, she chose to ignore them.

She closed the distance between them and reached out to touch his hand on the doorknob. Pulling it away slowly, she looked up into his eyes and said again, "Stay."

Chapter 7

"Roland." She whispered his name so softy she barely heard it herself.

He was in her bed, lying on his side, his chest bare, shoes off. His scent permeated the air, the rich, deep, musky aroma of his cologne. It would still be on her sheets in the morning. The indentation of where his head lay on the pillow would also remain once he was gone. Val knew she would cherish it all.

Nobody had been in this bed with her. Ever. The two attempts she'd made at a relationship had been with men who did not live on Grand Serenity. Both of them had resided on the neighboring island and she'd met them during the Anniversary—the weeklong celebration that commemorated the day each of the islands had gained its independence from the Netherlands. She'd visited them, but when they came to Grand Serenity it had been Val's decision to book a hotel room instead of bringing them here.

It had been easier to check in to a hotel under another name than to answer all the questions and stares that would undoubtedly come the moment one of the busybodies in her neighborhood saw one of those men. Funny how she hadn't given that scenario a moment's thought when she allowed Roland to bring her home. If his car hadn't been spotted by now, it certainly would be by morning. How was she going to deal with that? More importantly, how would he?

He stirred in his sleep, a little shudder and then a murmuring sound. She wondered if he were dreaming. Perhaps having a nightmare about his father. Her heart ached for him, and before she could stop herself she was scooting over in the bed, wrapping an arm around him. For the first few seconds she remained perfectly still, very aware that his skin was warm to the touch and his abs were hard as steel. Val rested her forehead on his back and matched her breathing to his.

What was she doing?

She had to be out of her mind. This was Prince Roland DeSaunters. He was not supposed to be in her bed and she was certainly not supposed to be touching him.

With that thought, she slowly began to pull her arm away, knowing it was necessary to retain some semblance of sanity. Roland, apparently did not feel the same way.

His strong fingers clasped her wrist in a gentle grasp and he slowly moved her arm back to where it had been, wrapped securely around his waist. He lowered his arm over hers and settled back into sleep. Val didn't know if she should say or do something, or just…go with it.

The latter won the battle, and before long she was drifting into slumber. She was all set to dream about her secret affair with the faceless knight in shining armor. It never occurred to her that the dream might not come tonight. Because she was already living it.

Today was a day for firsts.

Roland awakened in Valora's bed, alone.

It was a nice bed, he thought, even if it was a bit on the small side for him. He was used to king-size. The one in his cliff-house bedroom was a four-post California-king haven. He loved that bed and swore he could never get a real good night's sleep in any other one, even at the palace.

However, last night Roland had slept like a baby. He wasn't exaggerating, either. Even as he sat on the edge of the bed and wondered if Valora was in the kitchen or somewhere else around the house, he had to admit that he'd slept deeply and comfortably the whole night through. It was the oddest thing. The sheets weren't satin and quite possibly no more than three hundred count. He'd already noted the size. And there were too many pillows. Still, he'd slept well past his normal nine o'clock. That meant he'd had to rush.

Realizing that Valora was, indeed, gone, and cursing himself for sleeping so soundly, he pulled on his shirt and shoes. So she was gone. It was a weekday, she had to work, that was understandable. What was inexcusable was that he'd picked her up yesterday afternoon for their dinner date. He'd told her that he would take her back to her car when the date was over. The date had ended at her home, without her car. Roland had no idea how she'd gotten to work, but he felt like a total ass for not being the one to provide her transportation.

As he pulled out of her driveway, he could have sworn he saw two women duck behind some overgrown bushes. But Roland didn't have time to investigate. He was already running late. The car with the guards followed him into his own driveway and was ready to pull out twenty minutes later when he came back out. He drove directly to the palace where he had to run down the long first-floor hallway to make it to the conference room on time.

There were rooms designated for meetings all along the first floor of the palace; the bedrooms and private family rooms were on the second floor. Roland walked into the meeting behind two other gentlemen and took the empty chair at the foot of the table, right across from where Kris was already seated.

His brother looked at Roland as if he were a stranger off the streets.

"What are you doing here?" Kris asked in a hushed tone.

"It's the monthly cabinet meeting, correct?" Roland asked. "That's what the calendar said, and judging by all the people assembling, it was accurate."

"You never attend this meeting," Kris stated—as if Roland didn't already know that.

When a few of the cabinet members came over to speak to Roland and shake his hand, Kris had no choice but to abandon his surprise. That was just as well; Roland wasn't in the mood to explain himself any further.

Last night he'd made a decision. This morning he was acting on it. There was no need for a huge discussion about those facts. At least, none that Roland could see.

"Gentlemen," Kris said, his tone a little louder, as he was attempting to speak over the others who were talking in the conference room. "Let us take a seat so that we may begin."

They did, all twenty of the men and women who represented Grand Serenity's governing cabinet. It was a fact that Prince Rafe was the ruler of Grand Serenity, and Kris was his successor. But Grand Serenity was not a dictatorship. The cabinet was comprised of men and women from the military and elected officials of the island, and they were the persons who brought the concerns and needs of the people to the monarch to be addressed.

Roland knew each of them, not only because their names and photographs were displayed prominently alongside the royal family's in the City Center building, but because he saw them at events and sometimes when he was out and about around town.

"If everyone will look at the agenda which is in front of you, we can go down the list of things to discuss. Lunch will be served promptly at noon and then we will disperse," Kris instructed everyone.

The first hour of the meeting moved swiftly, with reports being given and minimal questions being asked. Roland followed along easily.

"In the matter of the new resort," Kris began.

"I have some thoughts about this," Roland said.

The entire room grew quiet.

Roland looked up to see that everyone seated at the

custom-made black walnut conference table now staring at him. He figured that right about now they'd all managed to get over the initial shock of seeing him there, but the fact that he was actually going to contribute to the meeting was stunning. He'd probably laugh about the looks on their faces later, but for now, he simply continued.

"The Moonlight Casino has seen a quadruple growth in its profits over the last year. Partnering with the cruise ships to offer excursions, including a cash-back incentive for each guest, has proved to be a fantastic idea on Sallinger's part. As such, the percentage of the island's profits from the casino should definitely be reconfigured in the coming year."

He'd pulled out his phone and swiped until he came to the notes app where he often jotted down things that he thought were interesting. It definitely wasn't like carrying a briefcase or dictating memos to a studious secretary, but for Roland it seemed appropriate.

"Now, I've done a little background research into Quirio Denton and his other properties. They're all profitable and located in well-visited tourist destinations. It makes sense that they want to add Grand Serenity to their stellar list. For us, however, this new resort also has to make sense.

"My suggestion is that we steer Denton away from the north side of the island and closer to the City Center and The Sunset. Instead of disturbing parts of our historic landscape, which a good majority of tourists come specifically to this island to see, why not add a four-star resort right next to the casino, the specialty shops and the city's thriving center, instead?

"We should be thinking of bigger and more accommodating ideas for these upcoming years. Now that we're receiving international cruise lines as well as the domestic voyages from North and South America, we should be working on a larger scale of entertainment."

He paused then, because he'd reached the end of his notes. Sitting back in his chair Roland looked around and asked, "Thoughts?"

Kris spoke first, astonishment clear in his tone, "You know about the Denton deal and the figures for the Moonlight's year-end profits?"

Roland smiled, this time because he was kind of enjoying throwing his serious, controlled and perfect brother off-kilter for a change.

"Despite what the rumors say, Your Highness, I do actually read the monthly reports your secretary sends me. I'm not a complete and total loser who wears a crown," he told his brother.

Kris rubbed a finger over his chin and shook his head slowly. "I never thought you were a loser, Roland. I also never thought I'd see the day when you decided to use the astute business brain I knew you had buried somewhere beneath the poker games and worldwide jaunts."

Roland chuckled. "Thanks, big brother."

Kris actually smiled back at him. Then the crown prince cleared his throat and immediately got back to business.

"Let's discuss Roland's suggestions. I think there's some good in them. What do you think?"

Roland pulled up a new screen in his notes app and began to type in some of the things the cabinet members were saying. When the meeting was over he felt damn good about being able to contribute, acting like a prince of this island in a way he never had before.

It was satisfying, he thought, just like sleeping in Valora's arms last night had been.

"He's not going to marry you, either."

Val was just about to walk out of the flower shop when she heard the cool words.

Today was Wednesday. Her mother, Michele Harrington, had died on a Wednesday, after giving birth to her. So this was the day that Val always picked up a small bouquet, which she put in the vase on her dining room table. This week the bouquet contained angel wing begonias. Her mother's favorite flower. Angeline Forigua owned the flower shop after inheriting it from her mother. It was Angeline's mother who had always created bouquets for Michele.

"Excuse me?" Val asked as she looked up from examining her bouquet.

The woman walked slowly, her high-heeled pewter-colored sandals clicking on the glossed cement floor. She wore a floor-length summer dress in a lovely nude shade with colorful butterflies. The chiffon material floated around her legs as she walked closer to Val. Diamonds sparkled at her ears, big fluffy curls bounced at her shoulders and everything about her said money, privilege, power.

"You heard me," Malayka said as she adjusted the cream-colored leather purse on her arm. "He will not marry you. Roland is not going to marry anyone. I would think, since your family spends so much time worrying about the goings-on at the palace, that you would already know this. Perhaps that's your angle," she continued with a tilt of her head.

"Maybe…" her voice softened as she touched a hand to the collar of Val's polo shirt "…you might be planning to use your feminine wiles on him."

Then she tossed her head back and laughed. Another woman standing at the front of the shop turned to look at them. Angeline, who was a short distance away behind the cash register, looked up, as well.

"I don't want to marry him," Val said, her fingers clenching around the green tissue paper that Angeline had wrapped the flowers in. "I'm not interested in a romantic relationship with Prince Roland, just as I wasn't interested in one with Prince Kristian."

Malayka's laughter subsided as she shook her head, a smile still affixed to her face.

"You don't fool me," she told Val. "I know exactly what type of woman you are. An opportunist."

"No. I'm not," Val replied as she tried her best to remain respectful. "You are mistaken."

"Oh, no, I'm not," Malayka argued, this time letting the smile slip. "I know that you're hungry for a crown and I don't blame you. That's why I'm glad I was here finalizing the flowers for my wedding and saw you to offer you a little advice."

Val wanted to say she didn't need her advice. She wanted to tell the woman to take the luck she'd had in snagging Prince Rafferty and go straight to the devil. But she did not.

"Stay in your lane," the soon-to-be princess told her. "The royal family…*my* family, is way out of your league. Don't forget that again."

Val could hear the paper crinkling in her hand as she squeezed the stems of those flowers even tighter. Her teeth clenched with the words she told herself she could not say. Then came a voice from behind her.

"Hello, Valora." Princess Samantha spoke. "It's nice to see you again. I was planning to pay you a visit to thank you for the support you offered my family last night."

Val turned slightly to see the princess standing there, dressed in a lovely peach-colored pantsuit. Her dark hair was pulled back into a high ponytail; small gold hoop earrings shone fashionably at her ears.

Val smiled. It was an easy action, as she was used to dealing with the public and regrouping quickly after strained situations. "Good afternoon, Your Highness," she said, and gave a quick curtsy.

"Oh, those flowers are lovely," the princess continued as she reached out a hand to touch the soft pink petal of a begonia. "Aren't these beautiful, Malayka? Have you asked Angeline about these type of flowers for the wedding?"

A quick glance at Malayka caught the woman rolling her eyes.

"I'm not interested in the ordinary and you're late," she snapped.

When the princess only tilted her head and arched her brows in response, Malayka continued, "I do not have much time. I need to get back to the palace to check on my prince. I've made all the final selections. You are welcome to have a look, but my decision is final."

Val hadn't noticed until the moment it rang that Malayka was holding her cell phone.

Malayka huffed as she lifted her hand and looked at the phone. "I have to take this. Don't be too long with this one," she said to Princess Samantha. "Like I said, I have to get going soon."

Without so much as a cursory glance in Val's direction, Malayka turned and walked away. Samantha gave a slight shake of her head as she visibly inhaled and exhaled slowly before turning to Val. She offered a smile, even though her body language screamed that she was anything but happy at the moment. Val had wondered, as she'd looked from Malayka to Samantha during their exchange, how two such different creatures could now be so very close to becoming family.

"Well, I guess that leaves us to look at flowers, doesn't it?" Samantha asked Val.

"Ah, no. I mean, I was just leaving when the pri… I mean, when she stopped me." Val knew she sounded ridiculous—stuttering and stammering over her words as if she'd never spoken to another human being before.

Val took a breath.

"Pardon me, Your Highness. I've been at work all day, giving the same tour speech over and over again. Real conversation seems to be beyond me at the moment." Val chuckled as she saw the princess continue to smile and nod.

"Don't worry about it," Samantha said. "Believe me, I know how daunting it can be to stand on your feet and talk all day. I've had plenty of days like that, myself."

"I'm not complaining," Val hurried to correct herself. "I love my job. I'm just saying that sometimes it makes me hard to communicate with. But I'm just going to go now before I embarrass myself anymore. It was a pleasure seeing you again, Your Highness."

Val hurried out of the flower shop before she could blabber any longer or embarrass herself any further. She was finally and thankfully at her car and about to get in by the time she could breathe a sigh of relief.

That was a moment too soon.

"Well. Well. Well. Look who made it out of the house today."

She didn't have to turn to know that it was Cora's voice she heard. Of all the people on this island that she could run into this afternoon, it had to be this one. After opening the driver's-side door Val turned slightly to see her father's ex standing not more than two feet away from her.

Cora wore ruby-red high-heeled sandals today. She wore heels every day to make up for her small stature. Her waist was slim in the fitted denim dress she wore, and the red silk scarf tied stylishly around her neck matched the matte lipstick on her lips. Her perfectly colored auburn hair was pulled into a neat bun at the back of her head.

"Hello, Ms. Cora," Val said, even though she feared she was dangerously close to losing all her manners today.

For that reason, she prayed this exchange with Cora would be short and sweet. To help facilitate that need, she leaned in to set her purse and her flowers on the passenger seat of her car. When she stood straight again, it was to see that Cora was still standing there.

"So you went to work today?"

Strange question, but Val didn't feel like wasting any more time.

"Yes, ma'am, I did. Just stopped by the flower shop to pick up my weekly bouquet and now I'm on my way home," Val told her, and jingled her car keys to show that she was about to get in and drive away.

Cora took a step forward. "You worked yesterday, too," she stated. "I know because my nephew and his wife are here visiting for their wedding anniversary. They came down to the museum and took one of your tours, just like I told them to."

"Oh, that's wonderful. I wish they would have told me they were related to you," Val said, trying valiantly to keep her smile in place.

If anyone had mentioned knowing Cora to her, Val would have made a point to ignore them the entire duration of the tour. Yes, that would have been rude, but she would have done it anyway, because this woman was one of her least favorite people in the entire world.

"Lorna Magens's girl, Tara, works at the hospital. Did you know that?" Cora asked as she leaned on Val's car and folded her arms over her chest.

"No. I didn't know that," Val replied. "I haven't seen Tara since she went off to college."

"Well, she's back now. Graduated and has a degree in nursing. That's why she works at the hospital."

"Okay. That's good for her," Val said, and then moved like she was about to put one foot in the car.

Cora came closer until she could drop her arms and wrap her fingers around the window part of the door that was still open.

"Tara said she saw you at the hospital last night.

You came in with Prince Roland, of all people. Now, I haven't heard a word about any of the royal family being at the hospital last night, so I wasn't about to believe what Tara said—until I rode past your house this morning."

Val did not reply.

"You don't have money to buy a car like that, and your father's as unlucky in gambling as he's managed to be in his sorry life, so I know he didn't buy it for you," Cora continued. Her fake eyelashes resembling spider's legs when she blinked.

"It wasn't my car," Val said simply, and then slipped into the driver's seat of her car.

She was about to pull the door closed when Cora stepped in the way.

"You aren't trying to get your clutches on the other prince, are you? Girl, you're just like your daddy. Delusional!" Cora snapped. "Your poor mama is probably turning over in her grave right now knowing what you're doing. It's disgraceful, Val."

"You're in my way, Ms. Cora," Val said as steadily as she could manage.

Her patience was wearing thin.

"I want you to listen to me, chile. And listen good," Cora continued.

Val shook her head after looking away to snap her seat belt in place. Cora was wagging a finger and about to tell her something Val knew for sure she didn't want to hear.

"No, Ms. Cora. I do not have time to listen to you today."

Before the woman could say another word, Val

pulled on the door bumping the woman until she finally had the good sense to get out of the way. When she was able to, Val slammed her door closed and started her car just as quickly as she could. She pulled out of the parking spot without even looking for oncoming traffic. Val just drove and prayed she'd make it to her destination safely. On second thought, what did it matter if she did or not? If this was all she ever had to look forward to in life...

Chapter 8

Val didn't curse. She didn't scream and she didn't get out of the car.

He was sitting on her front step, sitting on her welcome mat. Wearing a dove-gray suit, his jacket open so she could see the white dress shirt he wore beneath it and the cotton-candy-pink tie he'd undone but left hanging around his neck. On his feet were expensive shoes in a darker shade of gray, and his socks were gray with pink polka dots. A striking outfit for a striking man.

Why was he there again?

Why did the gods get such a kick out of making her life miserable?

"Sorry about that," he said when he opened her car door. "I should have immediately come to open the door for you. Please accept my apology."

Val jumped at the sound of his voice. She hadn't even realized he'd gotten up off the step and walked down the driveway. Now he was standing there holding the door open for her. His cologne was strong, or rather, the effect of the pleasantly sensual fragrance was potent. Enough to make her tremble before she gave herself an inward shake and a command to get it together, pronto!

"No need for an apology, Your—"

He held up a hand to stop her from speaking. "I know I've asked you this before, but since you were on your way to forgetting, let me remind you that we've slept in a bed together. That means it's okay for you to call me Roland."

She'd said his name before. Last night, as she'd watched him sleep, she'd whispered his name. And then in her dream. She still couldn't see her knight in shining armor's face, but she'd said *his* name. Roland.

She leaned over to the passenger seat and grabbed her purse and the flowers.

"Thank you, Roland." She spoke as she climbed out of the car.

He didn't back up, as he should have when she stood. In fact, he made no attempt to give her an inch of space to get away from him.

"I like this," he said, taking a step closer.

"You like what?" she whispered as she resisted the urge to back away.

He grinned. "Greeting you when you come home from work."

She shook her head and tried to look away. His eyes were too dark. The brown too intense. The edges of his beard too sharp and clean.

"I know how to open my car door for myself," she said, and felt instantly foolish and aroused the moment he took her chin between his fingers and tilted her head until she was staring up at him.

"I know," he said. "And you can drive, too. I've seen you do it."

This time, when she opened her mouth to reply, Roland took it. Moving in, his lips were on hers instantly, his tongue slipping easily inside to duel with hers as if he'd been waiting all day to do just that. Her fingers were crushing the plastic on the stems of her flowers again. He slipped one arm around her waist and pulled her close. She couldn't touch him. She wouldn't, even if she could. This was ridiculous.

She wanted to kiss him *and* to touch him.

Tilting her head, Val leaned into the kiss. It was good. Hot and spicy came to mind as his hand flattened on the curve of her bottom, the other one still possessively holding her chin. He sucked her tongue deeper into his mouth. Her legs trembled. He moved forward. She leaned back, vaguely feeling her back against the car. She moaned. It sounded so helpless. He ground his growing erection into her. She moaned once more.

"We should probably take this inside," he said, pulling his mouth from hers only long enough to say those words.

"We should…ah, probably…stop," she admitted and attempted to turn her face away from him.

It didn't matter. He began nipping her jaw. Tiny pricks of his teeth followed by warm strokes of his tongue. This was worse than the kiss because it felt better. So much better.

"Yes," she heard herself say.

"Yes," he echoed and began moving backward, pulling her with him.

"No." She shook her head. "No!"

At that, his hands instantly left her body. So quickly she almost fell. Of course, he caught her. He was a prince, after all. The prince always caught the—

What was she doing?

Val was not a princess and she definitely wasn't a damsel in distress. She was a grown woman, coming home after a long day's work, and she was ready to find some semblance of peace in her life.

After a steadying breath she turned and closed her car door. Pushing her purse up onto her shoulder, she gave a little shake of her head and tried to start again.

"Hello, Roland," she stated evenly, finally deciding she was together enough to look him in the eye once more. "Thank you for opening the door for me. It was a very chivalrous gesture."

Then she was moving, heading to her front door.

"However, I'm not sure what you're doing here. Oh, did you leave something behind this morning?" she asked and looked back at him.

"No," he replied and laughed when she bumped right into him as she turned.

"Oh," she said, not realizing he'd been following her that closely.

"I don't think I left anything. Still, there was this urge to return."

Val turned back. Her keys were in her hand. No, she thought as she looked down, they weren't. What the—

Roland was laughing again. She looked up to see him

jog back to the car, open the door and take her keys out of the ignition where she'd so foolishly left them. Feeling like a complete idiot—and still a little flushed from that sexy-as-hell kiss—Val put her hand out for the keys when he returned to her. Roland held them out of her reach and circled around to open the door.

"You don't even know which key it is," she insisted and felt even more inept as he opened the door.

"I have an excellent memory," he told her with another smile as he stepped to the side and gave a flourish of his arm to signal that she could now go inside.

For the second time in as many days, Val walked into her house like she was a guest. The memory of his letting her in last night was still fresh in her mind. That was, until she pushed it aside because the more pertinent memory was of Malayka and her father's ex telling her she was making a fool of herself with Roland.

"How's your father?" she asked after dropping her purse on her couch. Her steps continued just a few feet away to her dining area.

There was a vase there, still holding last week's flowers. Val carried the vase and her new flowers into the kitchen. She'd heard Roland close the door so she knew he would follow her.

"I just left the hospital," he said. "The procedure was earlier this afternoon and it went well. He was extremely agitated when he was in recovery so they sedated him. We'll get to talk to him tomorrow."

She'd been changing the water in the vase, dropping the old flowers into the trash and unwrapping the new ones to slip them slowly into the fresh water. When she finished she looked up at him.

He'd taken a seat at the short breakfast bar, on one of the stools she'd found at Mr. Tuda's antique shop last summer. After two days of sanding and four ibuprofen to get rid of the ache in her shoulder, she'd been able to paint the stools a cheery yellow to match the curtains in her kitchen.

He was staring at the flowers.

"I remember when my mother was in the hospital," he said. "I was only seven, but I remember sitting in a waiting room and one of the staff bringing me a cup of hot chocolate. I tried to drink it too fast and scorched my tongue. I cried and a nurse came over and picked me up. She took me into the room where my mother was and let me touch her hand. That was the last time I saw my mother alive."

Val's fingers shook on the vase. She was glad it was sitting on the small round table in the center of the kitchen floor, or she definitely would have dropped it.

"On the table beside the bed in that hospital room was a vase full of flowers. She loved fresh flowers and always had them throughout the palace," he continued.

"My mother loved flowers, too," Val told him. "My dad said she had a garden. It was in ruins by the time I was old enough to walk. But I have pictures, and I see her smiling proudly as she showed off her hard work. My dad used to give her bouquets of flowers when they were dating."

"So you buy bouquets of flowers as a way of remembering her," he said quietly.

She nodded. "What do you do to remember your mother?"

"I stay here," he answered. "I won't move away from

Grand Serenity permanently because everything I remember about her is here. She loved it here and would never leave, not even when the natives told her she had no business coming from another country trying to marrying into royalty."

"But you don't really want to be here, do you?" she asked. "You want to go far away, somewhere that nobody knows you're a prince."

"Where nobody knows that I'm supposed to act like a prince at all times. Walk like one, talk like one. All the things a prince does, except rule." He shrugged. "That's fine with me, because the last thing I want to do is be responsible for an entire island full of people. It's not what I'm cut out to do."

She nodded because she knew exactly how that felt. Val didn't believe she was meant to guide tours for the rest of her life. There was another yearning inside her, one she'd yet to fully grasp. She wondered if Roland had something he could reach for.

"I have leftover grilled chicken and macaroni salad from my dinner last night. I think there's enough for two," she announced, then lifted the vase and carried it back into the dining room.

When she turned it was to see that he was still seated, although he hadn't replied to her. That was probably better. She shouldn't have offered anyway. Why eat her leftovers when he had a cook who would prepare his favorite rice pudding the instant he asked?

"How was your day?" he asked when she went back into the kitchen.

"What?" she asked, momentarily confused.

Roland smiled. "Isn't that what people do after a

long day at work? They sit in the kitchen while dinner is being prepared and they ask each other how their day was. So, how was your day?"

That's what married people did. Val picked up on that instantly. Roland hadn't said those exact words, but she knew, and she shook her head to clear the thought away. She wasn't married to Roland.

"Three tours, one in the morning and two this afternoon. At lunch I sat in the atrium with my tuna sandwich. How about you? What was on your royal schedule today?"

She hadn't meant for it to sound sarcastic, but she knew it did. He wasn't an ordinary working person, like she was, and it didn't really make sense to act as if he was. Still, she felt bad. So she turned away from him, going to the refrigerator to pull out the leftovers.

"I went to a meeting this morning. I suggested we do something to increase tourism on the island. I think it might work," he told her.

"Are you on the tourism board, too?" she asked after setting the plastic containers on the counter. "I know the princess is very active on the board. We hear in our monthly meetings how the prince wants us to bring in bigger artists, feature more diverse exhibitions to draw in more visitors."

"The more stable our economy, the less chance we have of anyone trying to take over the island," he said.

"Is that even a possibility in this day and age?" she asked. "I mean, I know it happened before, when your grandfather and my grandfather fought to end Vansig's tyrannical reign. But we're different now. We've grown so much since then."

Roland shook his head. "We're an independent province, with a small military compared to the large countries surrounding us. Anything is possible."

He'd certainly hit the nail on the head with that statement. Anything was possible, which was why he was in her house about to share a meal with her.

"So, wait a minute," she said, just recalling what he'd said. "I thought you weren't into the business end of things."

"That's what everybody thinks," he told her. "Remember we were talking about misjudging before."

Okay, he was right. "I agree that people shouldn't rush to judge anyone else. But I can make assessments based on what I've been shown. I've never seen you at any of the board meetings at the museum. Your brother, your sister and sometimes even your father, but never you. The museum was one of your mother's famed projects on the island. I'd think if there were one thing you would do—if you were inclined to—it would be to make sure everything was as it should be there."

"The museum employs one hundred and fifty-seven islanders. Its annual revenue contributes three-point-four percent to Grand Serenity's economy. This year two new exhibits were introduced. With each opening there was a four percent increase in visitors and a one percent increase in annual subscriptions. The gift shop alone brings in almost seventeen percent more in retail sales compared with other gift shops throughout the island."

He was speaking in a normal tone, watching her watch him as he did. Again, Val felt foolish. She was also impressed.

"This will be the second time today I've had to explain that while I'm not seen at the meetings, that doesn't mean I don't read the financial reports that I'm always copied on. I know the status of every aspect of this island's growth. And because I'm the more social of the royal family, I even know a good number of the business owners personally," he informed her.

"And you keep all this hidden because…?" she asked as she finally remembered to put the bowl with the chicken into the microwave and start the warming process.

"It's always made sense to do so," was his reply. "Until now."

She'd leaned back then, her arms bent, hands grasping the edge of the counter. When he stood, Val wasn't sure what he was going to do. Was he leaving? Had she said too much? Made him feel uncomfortable? All of this was uncharted territory for her, so she felt like she might be in over her head when dealing with His Royal Highness.

"You want to know what *doesn't* make sense?" he asked.

He was crossing the short distance between them and Val's fingers instantly clenched the counter tighter. This wasn't going to be good.

"What's that?" she asked. Hearing her voice sound confident and steady was a terrific boost to the jumble of nerves dancing in the pit of her stomach. Why did this happen each time he looked at her the way he was looking at her now? Why did he insist on getting closer to her? Barging into her space?

"This morning was the first time I woke up in a woman's bed alone," he said simply.

Val opened her mouth, a sassy quip on the tip of her tongue. But Roland's finger lightly touching her lips put the comment on hold.

"When I walked into the conference room at the palace, that was the first council meeting I'd ever attended." His voice softened as his gaze fell to his finger. The finger that was now tracing the line of her lips.

She swallowed, her nails attempting to scratch into the laminate counter.

"Pulling up here and sitting on your step to wait for you was the first time in my entire life that I've actually waited for a woman," he continued.

His finger had made its way to the center of her bottom lip where it pressed lightly. Val didn't know what to do or say next. Apparently her body did, even if her mind was struggling to catch up.

Her tongue snaked out slowly until it touched the pad of his finger. His gaze instantly came to hers. The deep brown of his eyes grew darker, hungrier, and Val grew bolder. She closed her lips around his finger, suckling slowly until he pushed it farther into her mouth. Their gazes held as her mouth worked over the digit. His breathing grew faster, his lips parting, body moving until it brushed against hers. He was hard. She was aroused.

"You're the first woman to ever get to me," he whispered. "The very first one."

Val pulled her mouth away, loving how he immediately moved his hand to cup her bottom possessively, and the finger that had been in her mouth now lightly touched her chin.

"You're my first, too," she whispered. "My first dream."

Chapter 9

That was it. This had to be a dream.

It just had to be. There was no other explanation for Prince Roland standing in her kitchen, undoing the button of her pants and pushing them quickly down her legs. And if that part was a dream, the moment when she grabbed his face and brought his mouth back to hers was certainly from some sort of pleasure-induced slumber.

"Off," he murmured between kissing her and yanking at her clothes. "Now."

It took Val a second to realize that, no, this was not a dream, and yes, Roland really was trying to take her clothes off in her kitchen. With her entire body humming with arousal, there was no need to wonder what she was going to do next. Pressing her palms to his chest, she moved him back a couple of steps and then finished what he'd started.

Val toed off her boat shoes and pulled one leg, then the other out of her work pants. Because his hands had moved to cup her breasts when he whispered the word *off*, she grabbed the hem of her polo shirt and lifted it up and over her head. He made quick work of unsnapping the clasp in front that held her bra in place. In seconds it was sliding down her arms and hitting the floor. He was impatient, she thought with an inward smile. Why did she find that irresistible?

He'd taken his jacket off while she was removing her clothes, and his shirt was partially unbuttoned, but he'd stopped to help her with her bra. So chivalrous, he was.

Val finished unbuttoning his shirt while Roland cupped her breasts and rubbed his thumbs over her taut nipples. She bit her bottom lip to keep from groaning with the spikes of pleasure his touch sent soaring through her. His dress shirt and the tie that had been hanging around his neck went quickly. The T-shirt he wore beneath spoiled her anticipation of seeing his bare chest once again. So if she stretched it a little out of shape when she hurriedly pulled it over his head, Val wasn't going to let that bother her.

The belt buckle and the zipper of his pants were a little challenge, but Roland was all too helpful. She wanted his hands on her and her legs around him. Since when had she become so wanton? Val had no idea, nor did she care to try and analyze that fact. There would be time to ask and answer all of her questions. That time just wasn't now.

Roland took a little longer with his shoes and his pants, but he wasn't taking longer to undress. He'd slowed down to reach into his wallet and pull out a condom. Val thought she might just be falling in love with this guy.

He opened the wrapper slowly and sheathed himself in an even slower movement. Probably because her gaze had fallen to his shaft. Was her mouth hanging open at the glorious sight of him? Hopefully not. But he was definitely drool-worthy, all six feet and one inch of his honey-bronze body.

"Now?" he asked, his voice low and gruff.

Val looked up at him then and nodded. She licked her lips and spoke in a rush. "Now."

When he came to her and lifted her off the floor, sitting her on the counter and spreading her legs wide, the microwave timer beeped loudly. They both paused as if they'd been caught committing some crime.

He smiled and then she did, too. He grasped her thighs and leaned in to mouth her hungrily. Before the kiss was over, Roland was guiding his length into her center. Val was drowning in his kiss while sucking him deeper inside of her. She was wrapping her legs around his waist while wondering how and why this was happening.

When he tore his lips away from hers and pulled back until only the tip of his length remained inside of her before thrusting in quickly, deeply, once again, Val whispered his name.

She was still whispering it moments later as he pumped in and out of her so quickly and deliciously that her thighs trembled with her impending release.

* * *

With his eyes closed, his hands gripping her bottom and his head tilted back, Roland could swear he was in heaven. Or, at the very least, on a fast track to getting there.

When Valora had murmured his name and wrapped her arms and legs tightly around him, her entire body convulsing as her release overtook her, he'd been speechless. There'd been words, all of them rolling around in his mind: fantastic, warm, delicious, wet, need, more. He couldn't speak any of them, as they'd been running on loop since he'd seen her sitting in her car. Of course, he'd had no way of knowing how good this very moment was going to feel, but he'd guessed. He'd taken a gamble and he'd won. Oh, boy, had he won!

This was perfect. She was perfect.

He wanted to curse, but he refrained. Instead, Roland opened his eyes. She had leaned forward, with her forehead resting on his shoulder, and he lifted a hand to rub down the back of her head. Her hair was soft, just like the parts of her body he'd felt. And he felt like an idiot.

As gently as he could manage, Roland lifted her off the counter. Her legs remained clasped behind him as he walked them through the dining room and finally into her living room where he laid her on the couch. When she looked up at him, he saw confusion mixed with the look of pure satiation.

"You—" she began, but Roland only shook his head.

"I wanted to take care of you first," he replied before coming down over her.

She immediately laced her arms around his neck. He liked how it made him feel trapped there, with her and only her. He kissed the tip of her nose and then lightly brushed over her lips with his. They were soft. Was there any part of her that wasn't? He lifted one of her legs slowly, until he could prop it up on his shoulder. When he entered her this time, it was slow because he wanted to watch.

Roland stared down at her light skin tone. There was a series of freckles just beneath her right eye. Like someone had opened a bag and only spilled a few there. He wanted to kiss them. So he did. And then he eased into her, one excruciating inch at a time. She sighed at first, and then, when she realized he was staring at her, she grew quiet, tensing just a little.

"It's just me," he whispered. "Just me and just you."

Pressing farther into her Roland held her gaze. She sighed once more, her lips parting slightly.

"Just you and just me," he repeated and moved again.

Her eyes fluttered shut and slowly opened again.

"You like that, right?" he asked, hating the possibility that she might say no. "You and me. I like it, V. Do you?"

"Yes," she immediately replied in a husky whisper. "I like it."

Roland smiled, and then he moaned as he moved and enjoyed the feeling of being completely ensconced in her.

He rested his forehead on hers now, pumping slowly in and out. Closing his eyes, he relished this feeling, enjoying the slow and definite plunge he'd taken since deciding that he wanted her. It had been a slow revelation, taking him all of six days since their encounter on Friday night. That wasn't necessarily fast for Roland to decide he wanted to sleep with someone. What had taken hold quickly was the complete and forceful punch of possession that grew each time he stroked in and out of her.

She shifted beneath him, lifting up just a bit to lick the lobe of his ear. She said his name again and again, and he could feel her tightening around him. Roland gritted his teeth, trying with all that he possessed to stall the inevitable. It simply felt too good to stop, or to think of it ending. But the more she licked and kissed him, the more the warmth of her breath fanned over the damp spots her licks and kisses left, the deeper and deeper he fell, until he was done.

Moments later it occurred to him that he might be hurting her, so Roland mumbled an apology and moved so that she could stretch both her legs out on the couch. He still lay with her because he didn't want to leave, and the arm she'd kept locked behind his neck said she didn't want him to go, either. Just like last night.

They lay in silence for another few moments as Roland tried to figure out what should be said or done next. This was yet another first. He always knew what to say after sex.

Thanks.

That was great.

Whew.

Each of those phrases undoubtedly ended with him getting up and heading for a solo shower, which was followed by him getting dressed and leaving. It was a routine he'd perfected over the years.

This time, he was silent.

"That chicken is probably going to taste like rubber right about now," she said.

He laughed. He couldn't help it, and he wasn't sure if it was right or wrong, but it was natural and so he went with it.

"What?" she asked. "Don't tell me you like rubbery chicken, because that's just disgusting."

"I'll tell you what I like," Roland said after planting a very loud and wet kiss on her forehead. "A nice hot shower."

She smiled up at him and there was a quick tightening in his chest.

"That's great. I like those, too."

Chapter 10

They never did eat the chicken.

That was Roland's first thought when he rolled over onto his back the next morning. He was hungry.

And he was tired, but rejuvenated at the same time. He lifted his arms into the air and stretched his legs out while taking a big, noisy yawn. His fists hit the wall and his feet were chilly. He opened his eyes and realized why. He wasn't in his bed. Of course he wasn't, he recalled with a slow and satisfied smile. He was in V's bed. In her house. After spending the night.

After making love in her kitchen, they'd moved to the shower, where the small space and lukewarm water had forced them to stay close while they bathed.

Roland had stood behind her as she'd stepped under the spray of water, watching as fragrant white bubbles were washed away by clear rivulets of water. Her body was tight in every area, from the curve of her shoulder blades, down the line of her spine, over the hills of her plump bottom, down the stretch of her long legs. He hadn't been able to watch too long because his hands itched to touch.

She'd felt like warm silk as his palms moved from her waist down to her thighs.

"What are you doing?" she'd asked coyly.

"Helping to get the soap off of you," Roland had replied.

"I don't normally need any help," she'd said when he moved in closer, his awakening erection pressing inquisitively against the crease of her bottom.

"I don't normally shower with women," he'd replied.

When she'd turned slowly and met what he knew was his hungry gaze, Roland had to swallow hard. Her hair was wet, her face clear of any makeup, honesty brimming in her eyes.

"This is a first for both of us, then," she'd confessed.

Splaying his hands on her lower back, Roland had pulled her close to him. As if on his silent command, she'd reached her arms up to snake around his neck, tilting her head as if anticipating his kiss. He hadn't made her wait a second longer, but leaned in immediately and kissed her lips. Softly at first, then with an eagerness he'd never experienced before.

She'd tasted new and fresh, and somewhere in the dark recess of his mind a door opened and light spilled inside. There was a jolt inside him, one that Roland attempted to ignore.

"I'm happy to be your first," he recalled whispering after they'd made it out of the shower.

He'd gone into the kitchen then to retrieve their clothes. When he returned to her bedroom it was to see her standing by her bed, using the towel to dry her body. Without a word he'd removed another condom from his wallet, smoothing it over his length as she'd looked up to see him standing there.

She'd dropped the towel and stood there, gloriously naked, the last remnants of the sun dwindling in the window across from her bed. Her breasts were high, dark nipples puckered. The V of her juncture was neatly shaved until it almost appeared bare. Her toenails were painted a bright and vibrant red. Pearl studs were in her ears.

As he'd moved closer, she sat on the bed, then lay back, lifting her arms to welcome him. Roland had accepted the gesture, moving between her legs and slipping into her welcome heat, whispering into her ear over and over again.

"I'm glad to be your first. I'm so glad you're my first. So very, very glad."

They'd fallen asleep after another shower and a few moments of idle chatter as they lay in her bed cuddled together. And they'd slept soundly all night.

At least, Roland had. Just as he had in her bed the night before.

And, just like the morning before, he was waking in her bed alone. With a frown, he pushed the sheet that barely covered his midsection away and sat up on the side of the bed. His clothes were on a white wicker chair. His shoes were neatly lined up on the floor beneath them. The space was bright with daylight, the valance at her window allowing the outside in. It wasn't the view he had from his bedroom; Roland stood and went to the window anyway.

The street leading down this curving stretch of road to her house was cobblestone, as most of the streets in Old Serenity still were. There was a turnoff down a road that used to be grass but was now just tire tracks, and then there was her house. It was a strong structure that was probably one of the original dwellings on the island, but it was no palace. Better yet, it was no cliff house with a view of the mountains and a jaw-dropping fall to the sea. Yet he was comfortable there.

Noting that he was naked, Roland went to the chair and grabbed his clothes. He opened the door of her bedroom and crossed the small hall to the bathroom. All this was done without much thought, as if he was accustomed to being here. This was among the many things about his relationship with Valora Harrington that continued to perplex him, but Roland wasn't one to worry. There'd never been any reason to. Something either was or it wasn't. More often than not in his life, it wasn't, which was easy for him to digest.

Now there were uncertainties. As he splashed water on his face and used his finger to brush his teeth he realized that. He dressed in his pants and shirt, tucked his tie into the pocket of his suit jacket and decided to carry that to the car instead of wearing it. He wondered if it made sense to start packing an overnight bag. That spoke to some sort of permanency. He was smiling as he exited the bathroom, not sure why that thought had solicited the reaction.

The smiling ceased when he noticed a painting on the wall in the short hallway that led to the living room. He knew that place. It was the stretch of beach on the east side of the island that the cabinet had approved for use by cruise ships and their passengers. There were two other sections of beach on that side of the island, as well, but they served as venues for the paid excursions offered by the cruise lines. A very detailed deal had been worked out between the different companies, the tourism board and the ruling cabinet. Roland hadn't agreed with the idea of sectioning off the beach so that those with a little more money could enjoy a few more amenities while visiting the island. He felt that if everyone paid their fare for the cruise, and the cruise line then paid their fees to the island, then all was well and everyone could enjoy every part of Grand Serenity equally. But he hadn't bothered to attend that meeting or to voice his opinion. Now, staring at this picture that depicted the beach perfectly, had him wondering if he should have.

On instinct, he turned to the other wall and was rewarded with yet another painting. This one was a scene from the island, as well. These were the hills behind Serene Mountains. Roland took a step closer. He knew this spot because the Serene Mountains were the first thing he saw when he looked out of any window in his cliff house. This series of hills was covered in lush green grass with the crisp blue sky above, and in the distance, white sand beaches and the roll of the tropical seawater could be seen.

With a purposeful stride, Roland moved from the hallway to the living room where he recalled seeing more paintings when he'd walked into her house yesterday evening. There they were, a series of three paintings on the wall across from the area where she had a couch, a rocking chair and a small entertainment center. These three paintings were of another place Roland recognized. The palace.

Each one was a different view, one just as striking as the other. Sure, he was used to seeing this structure, as he'd lived there all his life, but this was different. These views, the way the light played off the gold-topped turrets and the seamless details like blades of grass bending in the breeze, were stunning.

As authentic as the paintings were, something nagged at Roland as he continued to stare at them. There was a connection, like a personal tug in the center of his gut as he looked from one to the other. Finally, he stepped closer to one and stared at it more closely.

"I don't sign the paintings," she said from behind him.

He'd thought she was gone and was momentarily startled to hear her voice. Still, he turned slowly, as if her presence had not just jolted him. "You painted this? You painted all of these?"

Roland knew he sounded incredulous. It was because that was exactly how he felt.

"Yes. I'm an artist," she informed him.

He watched with unfettered admiration as she squared her shoulders, daring him to say anything to the contrary.

"You're a phenomenal artist. These paintings are wonderful. Not only do they have depth, but there's so much emotion hovering over each one. It's amazing." He looked back at the trio on the wall.

"Thank you," she said and gave him a little smile.

"I thought you were gone," he told her when he looked at her once more. "Yesterday you left me here."

She was standing with her arms folded over her chest. After a few seconds she moved an arm, using her hand to smooth down the back of her hair. Then she dropped both arms and once again looked as if she were taking a specific stance. Roland wasn't sure what her body language meant at this moment, so he decided to wait and see how this was going to play out.

"Yesterday, I didn't know what to say to you," she told him.

And today she definitely knew what she wanted to say? Again, Roland waited.

She cleared her throat.

"I'm not one of you," she started, then shook her head. "No, that's wrong." She stopped and inhaled slowly.

Roland watched her. He noted the black leggings she wore with a loose-fitting white top that hit her at midthigh. On her feet were fluffy red socks that might have amused him if the atmosphere hadn't suddenly turned very tense.

She exhaled while flexing her fingers at her sides.

"I never intended for any of this to happen. Let me just make that very clear up front," she said, shaking her head. "This was not some plot contrived by me and my father to finally snag me a prince."

Roland relaxed his stance and slipped his hands into his front pockets. "Never thought you had."

How many times did he need to tell her that he'd already handled that situation with her father? Was she seriously still thinking that he thought this was some type of plot?

"Good," she said with a nod. "Thank you for that consideration."

"You're welcome," he replied.

Roland did not like this. As a rule, he tried not to predict anything. It was always best—for him, anyway—to simply go with the flow. Today, he wasn't so sure he liked the direction in which things were flowing.

"I've enjoyed the time we've spent together," she continued. "Immensely."

The last was added with a slight tilt of her lips. It was a hollow smile, one Roland didn't care for because of how sad it made her look.

"But I think we both know this is where it ends."

Her tone shifted now, to that of a cool businesswoman. Only Roland didn't do business, at least, not with women he slept with, particularly one he'd already begun to crave like some forbidden drug.

"I'm not sure I received that memo," he stated, opting to keep this as light as possible. Even though he was becoming more agitated by the moment.

"It's an impossibility," she told him. "You're a prince and I'm a painter."

"Just a few minutes ago you told me you were an artist," he quipped.

"You know what I mean."

Roland shook his head. "I don't, Valora. So why don't you just come straight out and say what you've planned to say to me? Isn't that what you've been doing in the time since you left me naked in your bed? Planning how this conversation was going to go?"

"There's nothing wrong with planning," she argued.

"To each their own," Roland replied with a shrug. Yes, he was really agitated now.

"This was good, Roland. But it will never work."

"I'm sure you have reasons for coming to that conclusion. I'd like to hear them," he said, knowing his voice sounded stern, possibly even cold. He wasn't in the mood to care right now.

"Well, for one, like I said, you're a prince. You're the brother of the first prince I was supposed to be engaged to."

He shook his head. "We've already been down this road. You know as well as I do that you and Kris were never really engaged. Try again."

For a moment she looked shocked. That quickly changed to irritation. Good, he thought. Let her see how she liked this feeling.

"I do not walk in the same social circles as you and your family. I'm not used to royal dinners, expensive gowns and traveling the world."

He shrugged. "I wasn't aware that I'd requested you do any of those things."

She folded her arms across her chest again, only to drop them quickly in a move that looked like it would only be complete if she stomped a foot and screamed. She did not, of course, which was a relief to Roland. She did, however, laugh.

It was an odd sound, considering the tone their conversation had taken, but Roland was past the point of surprise by now.

"The most obvious reason, if you even cared to know one thing about the type of person I am," she told him, "is that I don't do one-night stands. I'm not cut out to be a mistress or your chick on the side. When I begin sleeping with a man, I expect there to be some sort of commitment on both ends. I do not expect to wake up one morning a week later and see my lover in the arms of another woman. His next flavor of the week, so to speak."

And there was that. Roland hadn't given any thought to his other dalliances, not since seeing Valora topless and vulnerable in her father's house. He hadn't even considered how she must feel about that part of his reputation, because up until this moment, she'd never mentioned it. When he'd brought it up on the picnic, she'd brushed it right under the rug with the false rumors that were traveling around about her. Now she was voicing her concern, a very real and deep one, from the change in her tone.

"And another thing, I don't want to be kept a secret," she continued, and this time she crossed the distance between them to stand toe-to-toe with him. "I don't want to have to sneak around with the man I'm sleeping with, not anymore. If I'm going to be in a relationship with someone, it's going to be all-in or nothing. We're both going to work on a real and healthy relationship, or I'm not getting involved. That's what I deserve and that's all I'll accept."

He was quiet because he had no idea what to say. Of all the ways this conversation could have gone, Roland wasn't sure he'd imagined it going this way. Yes, he knew she was aiming at a "this has been nice but let's not kid ourselves" sort of speech, but in his own casual way he'd been prepared to tear that to shreds. The real, deep and valid reason she'd just stated for not wanting any part of him was something totally different. At least, for him.

"Exactly," she finally said with a shake of her head. "You don't know what to say because this is not your territory. You're not used to being the one left alone in bed, nor are you used to being approached with parameters and demands. It's always been Roland's way. Well, Your Highness, I'm sorry to inform you that I will not be taking any more trips on the Prince Roland Simon DeSaunters fun train. This is where I get off."

He was almost positive this hadn't been part of her plan, so when Valora stormed out of the room and he heard her bedroom door slam, Roland did not move.

He did not chase women. He'd never had to.

He did not give in to demands or make any concessions for the women in his life. Again, that hadn't been in his repertoire. So Roland did what he was used to doing. He made sure he had his car keys and his wallet in his pants pocket and his jacket still in hand, and he walked out her front door, closing it quietly behind him.

She didn't want him there anymore. That had come through all that she'd said and done loud and clear. So he would leave and he wouldn't come back, because Prince Roland Simon DeSaunters didn't have to convince a woman to want him.

Now, however, he did have to figure out a way to not to want Valora Harrington as badly as he still did.

"You look tired, son," Rafe said to Roland as they sat together by the pool.

He was actually exhausted.

After leaving Valora's house yesterday morning he'd

returned to his cliff house to take a long hot shower. When that failed to ease the turmoil inside him, he'd gone into his home gym and worked out for almost two hours. That was when his body screamed in agony and threatened to completely shut down if he didn't stop. Another shower, a bowl of rice pudding that had been left over from his picnic and a half gallon of water later and he'd felt somewhat normal.

He'd spent the remainder of the afternoon going through spreadsheets and financial projections, taking notes and trying desperately not to think of Valora. That evening, he hadn't fared as well. He'd lain in bed, wide-awake, until he was tired of lying there and not sleeping. For the duration of the night hours he'd sat in a recliner staring out at his mountains and thinking about his life.

The next morning, Roland had decided that he definitely needed to get out of the house. He'd taken a long drive, ending at the beach where he'd stood and watched the waves rolling in, remembering the day Valora had sat next to him, smiling and enjoying crab salad. Eventually, he'd ended up at the palace, where he lay back on a lounge chair across from his father, staring at the sparkling chlorinated water in the infinity pool.

"I'm fine, Dad," Roland replied to his father's keen observation. "It's good to see you up and around."

Rafe waved away Roland's words as he reached for the glass of lemonade on the small table between their chairs. He took a sip and returned the glass to the table.

"I told them I feel fine, too," he said. "But they insist I sit here and do nothing but stare out at the water.

The sun does feel good on my skin after being cooped up in the hospital these past couple days."

His father did look better. It seemed he'd lost a pound or two, but that could be because today he wore slacks and a polo shirt instead of the suit and tie Roland was used to seeing him in. Rafe was a stickler for being dressed for success at all times. *A leader should always look like he's prepared to lead*, he would say. Today, however, his father was the epitome of relaxation.

"The beach is so much better," Roland said.

He'd already admitted that today he was unwilling to stop thinking about Valora. Yesterday he'd sworn he was unable to stop the thoughts, but in the light of a new day he'd reconciled with the truth.

"Your mother thought so, too," Rafe replied. Then after a few seconds he continued. "Malayka doesn't like the sand."

"Two very different women," Roland told him. "Very, very different."

"I love her anyway," his father said.

Roland looked over to him. He wore sunglasses and his dark brown skin had a glossy sheen, which Roland figured was from the sunscreen his father wore.

"How do you know you love her?" Roland asked him.

Rafe folded his hands over his stomach.

"Because I can't stop thinking about her," his father replied simply. "The night after we met, I thought about her until the early-morning hours. I only knew her name but I had to see her again. It took hours for my assistant to find her in that hotel in New York. We had a late lunch that next day and dinner that night. That's how it started."

"Yes," Roland replied. He thought of a poker game, a sucky hand of cards and a misbuttoned blouse. "That's how it starts."

"I knew Malayka was not who anyone expected me to choose," Rafe continued. "She was everything your mother wasn't and as far from the royal palace as any woman could be. Yet she laughed at my jokes. Her nose didn't wrinkle at the smell of my cigar. Her hand fit perfectly into mine."

"Does it matter to you that we don't think she's going to fit perfectly here in the palace?" Roland asked his father the question that had been bothering him and his siblings the past months.

"Yes," Rafe answered. "Just as it bothers me that someone has been trying to harm us and is now on the loose. All of this bothers me, Roland. I know you may not understand how I deal with things, but it does bother me."

"I understand," Roland told him. "You just never thought I did."

"No, you're wrong, son," Rafe said as he turned his head in Roland's direction.

Roland met his father's gaze.

"I always knew you had the capacity to understand everything that went on in this palace. You were always a bright child. And unlike your brother and sister, you were adventurous and courageous to a fault. Every time I turned around you were jumping off some piece of furniture, riding your bike down the grand foyer stairs, breaking your arm and almost drowning when you were three and jumped into five feet of water."

Rafe chuckled.

"Your mother and I thought we'd surely die of fright each time you got out of bed in the morning. We had no idea what you were going to do, no matter how many nannies were hired to watch over you."

Roland smiled as he recalled some of his nannies.

"I always felt different than Kris and Sam," he admitted.

"You were different," Rafe told him. "Each of you were different and special. Your mother and I loved you so. When you lost her, I lost her, too."

"I know, Dad."

"These past few months have been really good to watch Kris and Sam find love. I know there's no other feeling like it."

"And you've found it again," Roland stated.

"Yes. I have."

He wondered how his father was going to feel when they proved that Malayka had something to do with the incidents that had taken place in the past few months. Would he feel as bereft as Roland did right now?

"You can find love, too, Roland," Rafe's words interrupted his thoughts.

"Excuse me?"

Rafe chuckled. "You heard me correctly," he said. "You can fall in love, too. There's a woman out there for you. If only you'd stop running long enough for her to catch up to you."

Roland frowned. "I'm not running."

"Oh, yes, you are," Rafe said as he turned back to

staring at the water. "You've been running all your life. But I think it's about time you slowed down. If you do, you might be surprised at who ends up standing next to you."

Nobody was standing next to Roland. Not a half hour after he'd left his father and was walking down one of the long hallways in the palace. He'd been looking at the paintings that hung in heavy gold frames throughout the fortress he'd once called home. Studying each portrait and landscape, looking for that burst of energy he'd seen in Valora's paintings. He hadn't found it.

Yet he did hear a sound toward the end of the hallway. Stepping away from the wall, Roland stared down to where the hall split in two directions. One went to the kitchens and the staff's quarters, and the other went to the doors leading to the palace storage facility. Considering a bomber had made his way inside the palace in the guise of a construction worker, Roland didn't think he was being silly at all when he saw a shadow going toward the storage area and decided to follow it.

He jogged down the length of the hallway, coming to a stop just in time to see one of the doors closing. Roland immediately moved in that direction, taking the three stairs that led to a lower level with ease. The scent of perfume alone was enough to alarm him. It was familiar. Expensive, abrasive with its tangy floral aroma. Malayka.

He wasn't just a man who loved women, he was a man who knew women very well. Even down to their perfume. Roland followed the scent.

She moved past the first couple of rooms, stopping at

the very end of the space and opening the last door. She stepped inside. Roland was only a few steps behind. It was dark in the room, but Malayka had not turned on the lights. Roland did that for her.

She gasped as she turned in surprise to stare at him.

"Did you forget something?" he asked.

Moving a hand to her chest—to cover her heart, Roland supposed—Malayka looked at him with irritation clear on her face.

"You're not funny," she told him. "Don't you have a poker game to play or some woman to screw? What are you doing down here?"

And so the gloves were off. Roland smiled. He was totally okay with that.

"Sure I do," he replied. "But I'd much rather see what you're up to."

She brushed down the front of her clothes—a pale blue jumpsuit with a gold chain belt at her waist—as if there were something on her. There wasn't, but he suspected she needed to do something, anything to keep his focus off what she was doing down there.

"I'm walking around my house, that's what I'm doing. Do you have a problem with that?"

When Roland only arched a brow at her she shook her head.

"Look, I don't care what you, your brother or your sister think. Your father and I are getting married, so the three of you might as well get used to it. You're all supposed to be adults. This running and telling Daddy that I'm the wicked stepmother is childish and unnecessary," she told him.

"Is it really?" he asked, keeping his gaze fixed on her.

She'd begun moving through the space. There were dozens of boxes stacked high along one wall. On the opposite side were shelves, five rows of them. More boxes and what looked like filled garbage bags were stored there.

"Yes, it is. Just like you sniffing around behind the woman your brother was supposed to marry is unscrupulous and just plain nasty."

After that insult, she pulled down a box and acted as if she were looking for something inside of it. Roland wasn't fooled for a minute. The last place in this entire palace that Malayka Sampson would willingly go was into these storage rooms. They were dank and cool and full of stuff they either no longer wanted or just couldn't figure out what to do with. So, what was the real reason she was down here? He planned to find out.

"You'll find that I can take insults just as well as I can dish them out," he said, and moved so that he was once again only a few inches away from her.

She looked up at him, her lips upturned and eyes narrowing.

"What do you want, Roland? Why are you down here?" she snapped.

"I want to know what you're up to," he told her.

"I'm looking for something if you don't mind."

"What would that be, Malayka? A detonator to the next bomb? Or perhaps your gloves, so you can tamper with another one of our cars?"

She shook her head and replaced the box she'd been going through. Grabbing another box, she didn't spare him a glance. "You don't even know how silly you sound. Why would I try to kill the man I'm going to marry?"

"That's a good question," he said, and was very proud of himself for resisting the urge to simply shake the truth out of this conniving woman.

"Right," she said, and whirled around to face him once more. "It is a good question and I've got one for you, too. You and your siblings think I'm after your father for his money and the title, but if that were the case, why would I try to kill him before I could get my hands on either?"

Roland didn't even blink. He, Kris and Sam had thought of that before. They hadn't come up with an answer. He wondered if Malayka was about to provide him with one.

"Why don't you explain that part to me," he told her. "And while you're at it, tell me how it is that your hairstylist, the man who was only allowed into the palace because of you, also turned out to be the mastermind behind the car accident, the bombing and the shooting, which was aimed at my sister?"

She didn't immediately respond.

Roland laughed.

"Come on, Malayka. I know you've got to have an answer for that one. A woman like you is all about planning. You don't leave out a detail or allow for any scenario changes. So why don't you go ahead and clear this up, once and for all."

There was silence for a few seconds. A sort of stand-off was taking place and Roland wasn't going to be the first to buckle. Malayka was first as she closed the distance between them and lifted a hand to lightly touch his cheek.

"What's the matter, Roland? You jealous because nobody's giving you any attention? Well, let me remedy that for you," she said, a slow smile spreading across her face.

Roland grabbed her wrist. "Don't. Touch. Me," he said through gritted teeth.

It was Malayka's turn to laugh. "Oh, don't kid yourself, baby. I would never make a move for a guy like you. Too insecure and immature for my tastes. That's why I fell in love with your father. Rafe's a real man. He not only knows how to lead a country, but he also knows how to treat a woman. That means he's not into sneaking in and out of a woman's house in the early-morning hours so that nobody will see him, and he certainly doesn't resort to meals on a dirty beach instead of taking me to a fine restaurant. Rafe gives me nothing but the best, from his personal and physical attention, to making sure that everyone, and I mean everyone, including his spoiled and selfish children, show me the respect I deserve."

Roland moved her hand away from his face and released his hold on her.

She continued to smile. "That's right," she told him. "Accept it. Just as you've had to accept you're always going to be second-best around here. Rafe is my prince and I'm going to be his princess. I'm going to make him happy because I love and cherish him. And one day, unfortunately, Kris will rule this island and his little wife will stand beside him. But where will you be, Roland? Standing on the sidelines, as usual. No real relationship.

No real duties to this island or the crown you wear by birthright only. Nothing. That's what you're going to have. So you keep following me around hoping to find something that's not there. It doesn't change a word of what I've said to you. Nothing will change the fact that you're a second-rate prince that's only good for a roll in the sack and not a thing more."

He took a step toward her and she quickly backed up. At his sides his fingers clenched as everything his parents had taught him about the opposite sex slammed into his brain. If she were a dude he would have slugged her. Later, he would regret stooping to that level, but he would have received great pleasure in connecting his fist to the jaw of the person who was disrespecting him. But this was a woman. It was Malayka, the woman who he still firmly believed was behind all the strange things that had happened, but a woman, nonetheless.

"When you fall, Malayka, I'm going to be right there. Looking down on you the same way you feel so privileged to do to others. Don't forget that," he told her. "Don't forget that I am here, second-rate, second-best, second born, whatever you want to call me. I'm here and I'm watching you."

"Get a life!" she snapped and pushed past him.

Roland shook his head and resisted the urge to laugh out loud. For, as smart as she thought she was, he was smarter. He wanted to see what she was looking for in this room. He needed her out of the room to do that, and he needed her to be the one to leave first. So he let her think she'd won this round, but she should have known better. Roland was the one used to winning.

Chapter 11

Sundays were made for gardening.

There was a picture of a beautiful bed of peonies and rosebushes buried in Val's top dresser drawer with those words handwritten on the back. It was her mother's handwriting. Michele had been in the picture, posing when she was five months pregnant with Val.

Now, Val used her Sundays to paint. She didn't have her mother's gift with flowers and plants. Instead, she used the talent she did have. It was therapeutic and encouraging, and she'd been looking forward to this moment alone since Thursday.

After Roland left her house that day, Val had changed her mind about not going to work. Instead, she'd dressed and headed to the museum. Her early tour had already been covered by another guide, so she had some free time until the afternoon bookings.

Val had spent that time walking around the museum looking at the paintings she'd come to love. Each one made her want to race home and pull out her own canvas to start a new painting. She had so many ideas, and the more she looked around, the more ideas came rushing to the surface.

For the next two days she'd gone to work, sketching on her lunch hours. At night, she'd perfected the sketches and checked her paints. Saturday morning before going in to work she'd visited the art supply store to stock up on what she could. Mr. Umberto did not have a stable supplier, as his sales weren't the best on Grand Serenity. There weren't many thriving artists here, so Val had to order most of her supplies online. She'd done that, but while she waited for them to arrive she knew she could start preparing her canvases.

Val had two ideas for paintings foremost in her mind, and they were both competing to get done first, so she was priming two canvases this afternoon and then she was going to select her background paint for each. The stark white color of the canvases wasn't going to work with the mood of the pictures she had in mind.

Soon her father had joined her outside. She was in the backyard because the gesso she used to prime had a strong scent that sometimes gave her headaches if she did not have proper air circulation. What could be better than open air on a gorgeous Sunday afternoon?

"You look like your mother standing there, so intent on your work," Hugo said as he came closer.

"Thanks," Val replied. She turned partially to look at him and then went right back to going through her box of paints. She preferred to use oils.

She hadn't seen or spoken to her father since the morning after the poker game in which he'd attempted to use her as payment. Even though he'd apologized to her then, his words had seemed empty, and Val was so tired of hearing them that she'd actually relished the silence between them. Now, looking up to see his bushy brows meeting as he frowned and the hunch in his shoulders made her feel like the world's worst daughter.

"I wanted to see you and to apologize again," he said before lifting a hand and scratching his head.

His hair, what was left of it, was slicked back with the same oil he'd been using all her life. It was too heavy for his thin hair and smelled like car grease.

"You don't have to say it again, Dad," she insisted.

He nodded and sighed. "I know I have many times before. But this time I want you to know I'm serious. I am sorry and I will not do that to you again."

Val was pretty sure she wanted to use the viridian hue for one of the paintings, so she dropped that and the other tube she'd been holding into the case and looked up at her father.

"You say that all the time, Dad and then you go and do something like it all over again. And, by the way, it's called lying," she informed him.

Her tone was harsh and she was sure the look on her face was, too, but she couldn't help it. Not only had her father been embarrassing her all of her life, but this time he'd walked her right into a mistake she feared would do more than ruin her reputation.

"I'm not going to lie again," he replied. "I can even

admit now that there was no engagement agreement. Well, not on behalf of the royal family, anyway."

His shirt was wrinkled. He said whenever he tried to iron, the hot device would inevitably rub against his protruding stomach—because, of course, he stood very close to the ironing board and usually ironed while only wearing his boxers. Val shook her head at the memory.

"I don't need to marry a prince. I'm okay on my own," she said, and then moved closer to straighten his collar.

"Alone is not good," Hugo announced. "I know because I hate every minute that I am alone."

"Dad," she whispered as she recalled how upset he'd been when she insisted on moving out and finding her own place when she was twenty-one.

Four years later, Val thought it had been the best decision of her life. Hugo, on the other hand, was still hurt by her move.

"I mean that I hate every minute your mother is not with me," he corrected. "She was my everything. I have never loved anyone like I loved Michele, and our love was beautiful. Every second that we had together was the absolute best. I want that for you."

Val could only nod because she wanted that for herself, as well. That thought had only surfaced in the last couple of days. After she'd told Roland that she wanted more than to be someone's lover, she'd started to think of how true those words actually were for her.

"I'll have it, Dad. One day, I'm sure of it."

She was sure. One day the right man for her was going to come along and sweep her right off her feet, just like in her dream. Of course, first she'd have to get over the fact that she'd already begun to fall in love with Roland.

Roland listened to Gary talk while he drove. His cell was on speakerphone, his fingers grasping the steering wheel tightly. He'd slowed down since receiving the call, because even he knew that it wasn't healthy to push the speed of his sports car while listening to his brother-in-law talk about the woman they all knew was out to get their family.

"From what I've heard from the guards, she's been sticking close to the palace and to the prince since he was released from the hospital," Gary told him.

"Really?" Roland questioned. "No more impromptu trips to the States? No more cryptic emails?"

"None," Gary replied. "I would say it's odd, but for a woman who is getting married in three weeks, it makes sense that her attention is focused on her fiancé and her wedding."

"Right, the wedding." Roland didn't bother to hide the edge in his tone at the mention of the big royal wedding. "I presume she's been receiving more deliveries to the palace. Things for the wedding that are going down to that storage room."

He could hear papers shuffling and figured that Gary must be in the office he used at the palace.

"Yeah, I have delivery receipts for six boxes earlier today. After you told me about your encounter with her down there and the number of boxes you saw, I decided to start monitoring all the deliveries myself. The guards had been keeping a log and checking out each deliveryman and their company, but I wanted to have a look myself. I agree, there are just too many boxes down there, and while it looks like fake flowers and linens and other wedding decor, it does seem like way too much. Especially since she could easily have an event planner taking care of all of this. There's no reason she should be accepting all these deliveries herself. I don't care how controlling she seems. Any woman with money and resources at her disposal like Malayka has would be sitting back allowing others to do all this grunt work."

"That's exactly what I thought," Roland agreed. "So, what was in the new boxes?"

"Drapes," Gary said. "Custom-made drapes. I instructed the staff not to accept any deliveries over the weekend, hoping to derail something in particular. So first thing this morning, a truck was granted access and came through the security gates. One of the guards signed for the package after inspecting the delivery truck and the driver. I found that the delivery slip was originally dated for Saturday."

"And when they couldn't deliver it on Saturday, they came back first thing Monday morning," Roland said as he made a turn onto a familiar street.

"Correct," Gary replied. "The guard called me and I came down to inspect the boxes before alerting Malayka to their arrival. She instructed the staff to take them to her storage room."

Her storage room. The sound of it irritated Roland even more.

"You said you found something in the financial statements?" Gary asked, switching the subject.

"I did," Roland replied. "I know Kris is up-to-date on all the banking business. But I also know my dad told him not to worry about those accounts with the Vansig name. Kris was still concerned. I'm glad I decided to take a look to keep my father from coming down on Kris for spending his time on the project. I don't know what it all means just yet, but I'm going to email them to you. Pay close attention to the highlighted portions and then let me know what you think."

"Will do," Gary said. "Be sure to send them through the special secured accounts I set up for everyone."

"No problem," Roland told him. "After all that's been going on I deleted all my other accounts. Expect them in the next fifteen minutes."

"Cool," Gary responded. "And I'll see you at dinner tonight?"

Roland made another turn and thought about what his brother-in-law had just asked. "Ah, no. Not tonight. But I'll be there by noon tomorrow, in time for our final fittings."

"Yes, the final tuxedo fittings." Gary sounded as excited as Roland did about that. "Three weeks until the big day."

"Three weeks to *stop* the *big day*," Roland replied.

"Problem is, I don't think we're the only ones counting down for that reason."

Roland agreed as he ended the call. He had to admit that he liked Gary Montgomery. Although he hadn't been terribly excited about handing over the care of his sister to an American, he couldn't ignore the fact that Gary was a soldier, just as Roland had been. Even though Roland was certain that his years with the Royal Seaside Navy were vastly different from Gary's time with the United States Army, he respected the military connection just the same. Besides that, Gary loved Sam and she loved him. Their emotional connection was undeniable. It was also enviable.

Kris and Landry's relationship was, too. Together, the foursome were a big part of the reason Roland hadn't spent a night in the palace for the past month. The feeling he continuously had—that aching in the center of his chest that he knew wasn't physical, but more emotional—each time he saw his brother and sister with their spouses. The nights he'd been unable to sleep, the rice pudding that had lost its taste because he couldn't stop thinking about the day he'd enjoyed it with her. The first picnic he'd ever had on a beach. The first night he'd spent with a woman wrapped in his arms, in her house.

Roland parked his car and sat there, wondering.

Why was he here?

When he'd climbed into his car it had been with the intention of riding the winding roads around the mountain, possibly getting out and walking along the cliffs. He loved the air there. Sure, the views were magnificent, but the air was fresh and crisp and rejuvenating. He'd needed something to kick-start him again. The text messages inviting him to another poker game weren't appealing. Eating wasn't appealing. Driving was becoming a necessity. What the hell was wrong with him?

She was home. Her red compact car was parked right in front of her home. It seemed in good condition, just as her house was. She took care of herself and her belongings. Independent and attractive. Why hadn't some lucky guy snatched her up already? The instant sting of jealousy circling the pit of his stomach at that thought almost made him laugh.

What the hell was he doing?

This wasn't like him. It wasn't like Roland...the Reckless Royal...to be indecisive. He wanted this woman. He'd had her. That should have been it. Yet, there was something else. A something that had guided his car back to the house he'd left three days ago with the intention to never return.

She'd said it couldn't be. *They* couldn't be...

Roland removed his keys from the ignition and stepped out of his car. He walked up to the front door. The blue door that, for some reason, made him smile. There were colorful homes throughout Grand Serenity, so this vibrant shade of blue should not have caused any reaction. But it did. When he reached up his hand to knock, it was with purpose. He'd made up his mind.

And once Roland DeSaunters made up his mind about something, there was no stopping him.

"Oh," she said when she opened the door.

"Hello to you too." He greeted her with a smile, then leaned in quickly and kissed her on the cheek.

He was walking inside before she had a chance to invite him in.

"I was working today and suddenly remembered I was hungry," Roland said as he moved into the living room and took a seat on her couch. "That led me to recall being offered some chicken and macaroni salad. However, I don't believe I ever had the chance to partake."

She'd closed the door and walked slowly until she stood a few feet away from him.

"What are you doing here, Roland?"

"I'm collecting on a dinner offer," he replied.

She shook her head. "I threw that chicken out and the macaroni salad is gone."

He nodded. "Okay, well, what else do you have?"

"Nothing," she said with a shrug. "I hadn't decided what I was having for dinner yet, so I haven't cooked."

"That's cool." He stood to walk toward the kitchen. "We can cook something together."

"What? Where are you going?"

Roland heard her talking, but he kept walking.

"I don't know why you're here, Roland, or what you're trying to do, but—"

He stopped walking and turned quickly because he knew she'd followed him and would be right behind him. She was, and he slipped his arm easily around her waist, effectively cutting off her words.

"But I can't stop thinking about you," he said. "Tell me you're not having the same problem. Tell me that those two nights we spent together, that first kiss, the first touch…tell me all of that meant nothing to you. That you haven't lain in your bed every night since then wondering what could have been."

She'd looked up at him the moment he touched her. She hadn't touched him. Her arms remained down at her sides, but her eyes, they couldn't look away. Her lips parted slightly as if she were going to speak at any moment. Or was it because she wanted to be kissed? He hoped so, because he was dying to kiss her. Holding on to what was left of his manners and waiting for her to give him the okay was slow torture. Roland would have sworn he was the royal who had it all together, but Valora Harrington had weakened him. She'd chipped at the facade and Roland doubted she even knew that she had, or how serious that act was turning out to be.

"It's not a good idea," she finally whispered. "No matter what I want, what I feel, what... I dream."

The last was spoken so softly, if Roland weren't standing so close to her he might not have heard it.

"I dream of you, too," he admitted. "Vividly. Every night. It's you and me and nobody else. Nothing else. Just us."

She was shaking her head now. "No, Roland."

"Yes," he told her as he leaned his face closer to hers. "Yes."

"It's impossible," she insisted when her hands came up to grasp his arms.

"Nothing," he whispered while rubbing his cheek against hers. "Nothing is impossible, baby. If we want it, we can have it. Just tell me you want it."

She leaned into him but shook her head again.

"Just say the words, V," he insisted as he inhaled deeply.

He loved the scent of her hair. It was fresh and sweet. Their bodies seemed to fit so perfectly, no matter what position they were in.

"Just say it," Roland implored once more, his fingers tingling as they gripped the material of her dress. "Please, just say it."

"Roland, I—"

The knock at the door seemed extra loud. Valora jumped and immediately pulled away from him as if they'd been caught doing something illegal. She looked as if she were about to be tried and sentenced, and Roland was instantly irritated.

"Valora Michele Harrington you open up this door

right this moment!" A woman yelled. "I know you're in there, so you just need to come on out here and let me speak my piece!"

"Who is that?" Roland asked.

Valora stood perfectly still staring from the door to Roland. Back and forth until she finally stepped toward him and put her palms on his chest.

"Go back in the kitchen and wait for me to take care of this," she whispered to him.

"What? No. Who's that at the—"

"Listen to me this time, Roland. Just stay here and let me handle this," she said through gritted teeth. "If I mean anything to you, just…please."

He didn't like it. Not at all. But Roland lifted his hands in defeat and took a few steps backward until he was completely in her kitchen. When she continued to stare at him, he even leaned against her counter and folded his arms over his chest. "It's your house," he told her. "Do what you need to do."

"Thank you," she whispered after a second of hesitation. "Thank you."

Chapter 12

"Curse you, Valora Harrington!" Cora screamed the moment Val opened the door.

"Shame! Shame! Shame on you!" Idelle, Cora's trusty sidekick came bustling into Val's house right behind her very riled-up friend.

This was the second time today people had come into her house without an invite. Val closed the door behind them with critical words burning her tongue. She wanted to get this visit over with as quickly as possible. Then she could go back to the other surprise visitor and...she had no idea what she was going to do about him.

"Hello, ladies," Val said to them as she went to stand beneath the archway that led from the kitchen into the dining room.

She wanted to make sure she put space between them

and the prince. The last thing he needed was to be found in her house. Especially by these two.

"What can I do for you today?"

"You can stop running around here acting like a harlot!" Cora shouted. "Didn't I warn you last week? But no, you didn't want to listen to me. Just kept on pushing your way into that palace and now look what you've done."

"A crying shame, that's what it is," Idelle said, her words sounding exactly like something Cora would say. "Now your daddy's out there trying to defend you and getting beat up in the process."

"What?" Val asked suddenly.

She'd been barely listening to the women because they never said anything she wanted to hear. She'd had no choice except to let them in, but she'd been determined not to let them upset her. Until now.

"What happened to my father?" she asked them.

Idelle's very thin, bright-painted lips snapped shut, as if she'd said something wrong. But that wouldn't have been the first time. Cora shook her head, the auburn hair hanging down today in big fat curls.

"You're so busy chasing men, you don't even know that your father got his face busted up last night by some man in a bar. That man had the audacity to say something about you trying to be Prince Roland's next conquest," Cora snapped.

"As if the prince would actually want to be bothered with his brother's leftovers," Idelle added, her voice only a fraction lower than Cora's.

Val gritted her teeth and took a step toward Cora. "Tell me what happened to my father."

The woman huffed, the action almost making the extreme amount of cleavage on display in her torso-hugging green-and-white dress topple out.

"He was down at Jen's Bar, getting drunk like he normally does, and then he starts trading words with this younger guy. Before anybody could really tell what was going on, your father yelled something about the DeSaunterses being a good family and Prince Rafferty being a better leader than anyone before him. The guy yelled back that no matter how much Hugo kissed up to the royal family none of those men were ever going to marry you, and Hugo slugged him." Cora shook her head then. "From what I heard, that was the best lick Hugo got in the entire fight. When Jen's daddy dragged Hugo out to his car, he said his face was swollen up like a balloon."

"Oh, no. Why didn't he call me? Why didn't somebody call me last night and tell me what had happened to him?" Val moved immediately to grab her phone so she could call her father. But Cora stepped in front of the small table that held her house phone.

"Now just wait a minute," she said touching a hand to Val's shoulder.

It was a stronger touch than Val would have expected and she took a step back to keep from falling.

"You're the cause of everything he's going through right now. If you'd stop wandering around popping up everywhere the royal family is—even going as far as to fake like something is wrong down at the museum so that Prince Roland would have no choice but to come down there and check on the place…you might avoid losing your job," she blasted Val.

"And getting people to park fancy cars outside your house to make it look like somebody rich is in here with you," Idelle interrupted with a hearty shake of her head. "Just plain despicable."

"Exactly," Cora agreed with her counterpart. "And whose car is that anyway? Why are they playing this game with you? You know there's gonna be hell to pay when Prince Rafferty gets tired of this nonsense. You know he's trying to plan his wedding and he has no time for foolishness like this from you and your father."

"That's precisely what I was about to tell you two ladies," Roland said from behind Val.

Idelle's eyes grew so big that Val thought for sure they would pop right out of their sockets like a cartoon character's. Then the woman immediately fell into a deep curtsy, bowing her head so her bulging eyes were no longer visible. Cora showed her surprise in a much classier fashion. After she closed her gaping mouth, she made a lavish curtsy, coming up slowly and inhaling deeply to assure her cleavage was even more visible.

Both women were murmuring "Your Highness," when Val turned to look briefly at Roland, who was now standing right beside her, before she moved to push Cora out of the way so she could get to her phone.

She was dialing her father's number when she heard Roland speak. "While I appreciate you ladies trying to protect my family's reputation, you should know that the vehicle parked outside is my car. And that I drove here today to see Ms. Harrington. Not to discuss her father or anyone in my family. I was actually looking for a dinner date. But as she obviously now has something else she must take care of, I'll ask you to excuse us while we ensure that her father is okay."

Hugo's phone was just ringing but there was no answer, so Val hung up and immediately made a move to get her purse off the chair so that she could leave. They could all keep standing right here talking about whatever for all she cared. She was going to go find her father.

Roland, however, must've had another plan. He took her hand in his and once again stood beside her.

"Well," Cora said, her gaze going down to their hands, then up again to Roland's face.

She didn't speak to him, but instead looked to Val as she whispered, "It's not proper. People will continue to talk about this."

"They can direct their concerns to me," Roland told her. "Be sure to tell them that."

"Yes, Your Highness," Idelle said with a nod of her head just before she started pulling on Cora's arm. "Come on. Come on," she said.

Cora was smiling at Roland, who had looked away from her to stare down at Val.

"Were you able to reach him?" he asked.

"No," she replied.

"Then I'll drive you to his house right now," he told her.

They were at the door only seconds after Cora and Idelle had made it through. Val grabbed her purse on the way and asked Roland to turn the small lever on the door so that it would lock once they were out.

Roland remembered where Hugo Harrington lived. He'd been to the man's house twice since the night of their last poker game. He hadn't expected to return to the dwelling, but tonight was an exception.

Valora had been silent as she sat in the passenger seat looking out the window. When he reached out a hand to hold hers, she'd accepted, letting her hand sit comfortably in his. But she still did not speak and did not look at him.

When he finally pulled into a parking spot, she pulled away from him and released her seat belt. The moment the car was turned off, she was opening the door. Roland hurried out and around to the curb to close the door. He fell into step behind her as she made her way to her father's front door. Apparently she had a key to Hugo's place, because she reached into her purse. When she found it, Roland reached out to take the keys. For a moment she hesitated, and then she just let him take it, asking him to hurry.

He did, and before she could say another word the door was open and Roland was stepping inside ahead of her. When he found a light and gestured to her, she moved inside, immediately calling out to her father.

"Dad! Dad, are you here?"

There was nothing.

Her cries grew louder, and Roland started to walk around the house, following her closely. Then Val went toward the back room where they'd played cards while Roland took the stairs.

"Hugo?" he called as he knocked on a closed door.

When there was no response, Roland opened the door. He had to walk inside to find a light but when the space was illuminated he saw there was no one there. On to the next room and then the bathroom. He was just about to leave when he heard a shuffling sound. Acting on instinct alone, Roland decided to stop calling to Hugo and he didn't call down to Valora, either. Someone was up here and he wanted to know who it was before he possibly put her in harm's way.

He heard the scratching sound again and looked up. There was a cord hanging from the ceiling and Roland pulled on it. Steps unfolded and he climbed them to the attic. It was dim but not totally dark, as there were two circular windows that reminded him of the portals on the navy ships he worked on. It wasn't quite night yet, but the sun had already set. The waning light cast throughout the space gave Roland a glimpse of rundown black shoes.

"Hugo?" he called out. "It's me, Roland."

There was silence and then movement. Hugo pulled his feet out of the light before whispering, "What are you doing here? You said I didn't owe you a dime."

Roland held on to his sigh of relief, but climbed farther into the attic. He wasn't exactly dressed for this today, wearing slacks and a button-front shirt, but he did it anyway. There wasn't enough room for him to stand up straight, so he bent forward and walked in the direction of those shoes. The closer he came, the more of Hugo Harrington he could see lying with his back propped against the wall. Roland bit back a curse.

"Do you need to go to the hospital?" Roland asked him.

"No," Hugo answered immediately.

"Why are you up here instead of in your bed with some ice on your face?"

"Because I don't want to lay in bed," Hugo snapped.

"Wrong," Roland said and knelt close to Hugo.

He reached out and touched the arm that he noticed the man was holding close to his chest. Hugo yelled out.

"Dad!" Roland heard Valora yell as she started climbing the steps. "Are you up there?"

"Don't let her see me like this," Hugo implored. He'd leaned forward so more of his battered and bruised face was visible to Roland. "I can't take it if she sees me like this. That's why I came up here."

Hugo was using his good hand to tug on Roland's arm.

"Take her downstairs. Please," Hugo insisted.

"If I do, when I come back up you're going to tell me everything that happened and then you're going to let me take you to the hospital."

"No," Hugo shook his head. "You can't take me."

Roland was about to pull away from him, but Hugo held on to his arm.

"I mean, call and have your people come and pick me up. I'll go, but I don't want her to have to deal with it. I want you to stay with her. Keep her safe," Hugo told him. "Please keep her safe."

Roland didn't understand why the man was asking him to keep Val safe, but he did pick up on the love in Hugo's voice. For whatever reason, he was afraid for Valora's safety. That was enough for Roland. For now.

He moved from the corner and stopped Valora before she could get to her father. As they were both bending over, it wasn't hard to shield Hugo from his daughter.

"Let's go back downstairs," he told her and reached for her hand.

She pulled away and asked, "Are you crazy? My father's over there and he's hurt. I'm not leaving him."

Roland hadn't expected any other reaction from her.

"I know that," he told her. "That's why we're going to go downstairs and call for an ambulance."

"It's that bad?" she asked. "I need to see him."

"Look, it's uncomfortable up here for all of us. Let's just go downstairs and make the call. The sooner we do, the sooner they get here and can help him. That's the most important thing, right?"

He hoped that little bit of reverse psychology worked. Valora was stubborn, and considering the women she'd just dealt with, not in a very good mood. There was a chance she'd push Roland to the side and get to her father anyway.

"What if he can't get down on his own?" she asked. The hurt in her voice was like a punch to Roland's gut.

He touched her shoulders. "I'll help him. Let me just get you downstairs safely and then we can make the call. It's all going to be fine, trust me."

She hesitated, and Roland recognized the hurt he'd heard in her voice. He now felt it, too, from the way she'd hesitated at his words.

"Just let me take care of this, Valora. I'll get your father the help he needs and then you can see to him," he said. Now was not the time to explore why Val's not trusting him was such a big deal.

She surprised him, and probably herself, when she turned. "We'll be right back with help, Dad," she yelled to Hugo as she headed for the steps.

Once they were both down in the hallway, Roland pulled his cell phone out of his pocket. He made a call to Brunson, who he knew would be parked right outside, telling the man that they needed a car and a medic, not the ambulance with its blaring lights and noise. Neighbors would see that and no doubt begin talking. He figured that was the last thing Hugo wanted right now, more gossip swirling around about him or his daughter.

"Thank you," she told him when he completed the call.

"Don't," he replied. "I'm just doing what's right."

Val opened her mouth and looked as if she wanted to say something but quickly closed it again. He was thankful she had. He knew that he couldn't take another blow like the trust thing again, so it was better if they just took care of her father for now.

"You should go downstairs and wait at the door for the car. When they get here, send them up. I'll wait with him until then," he said.

She still looked like she wanted to say something, but nodded, instead. Sighing, Roland headed back up to the attic.

"Alright," he said to Hugo as soon as he'd moved to the corner where the man was still sitting. "What the hell happened to you, and why do you think Valora isn't safe?"

"He told me she wasn't," Hugo said with a shake of his head.

Roland leaned in close to the man and asked, "Who told you that?"

"The guy that put his boot in my face. The one that used to work at the palace for the princess-to-be," Hugo said.

Roland didn't even question how Hugo knew who

worked where in the royal household. The man had made it his business to try and get his daughter married into their family; of course he would know everything about his family.

Roland was much more concerned with who Hugo was actually talking about.

"You said he used to work there. Are you talking about Amari Taylor?" Roland asked and held his breath waiting for the answer.

"Yes," Hugo said. "But that's not his real name."

Chapter 13

"So the fight wasn't about me?" Val asked Roland when they arrived at his house an hour after leaving her father at the hospital.

She hadn't seen him. Roland had taken her to his car and was already driving away when the transport he'd called for arrived and the guards who worked for him had gone into the house to get her father. He'd said they would all meet at the hospital, and they had. There was no way they could have known that the doctors would be so eager to look at her father's injuries that they would go down to the emergency room entrance. She figured that's probably what happened whenever the prince called in to the hospital personally and requested assistance.

Twenty minutes later the doctors had come to the waiting room to say they would have to operate on his arm and that he would probably remain heavily sedated throughout the night. They'd suggested she go home and get some rest and come back in the morning.

Val had been insistent that she would never get a moment's rest at home and that she would prefer to stay at the hospital. Roland had announced that he would take care of her. That obviously entailed bringing her to a lovely house on the cliffs. In all her years living on this island, Val had never been inside one of the houses that were nestled quaintly into the mountainside. And she'd certainly never expected any of them to look this good.

The winding roads brought them up the mountain, where the lush green landscape seemed to split open, giving way to light rocks and a contemporary white haven perched right on the cliff's edge. Inside was a blend of sleek and natural designs, from the light wood floors to the glass dining room table and the heather-gray couches with darker gray pillows.

There was a sitting area that she was particularly drawn to and Val immediately walked there when Roland instructed her to make herself at home. It was on the other side of the living room, where the floor-to-ceiling windows stretched into a quaint little area. There were two oddly shaped chairs there, and deep-cushioned black leather chairs. They were positioned with their backs to the window, so that the occupant could benefit from the suspended gas fireplace just a few feet away. The fireplace was the eye-catcher here, with its hammered steel casing. Val did not sit but, instead, stood there staring as Roland started a fire with the flick of a switch.

When he was finished he came around to where she stood and finally took a moment to answer her question.

"Not entirely," he replied. "Your father and this man apparently knew each other from years ago. They exchanged words about Hugo's continued attempts at connecting to my family. Like those ladies that visited your house earlier were saying, word is spreading around the island about you and me. Your father, of course, defended your honor. The man did not like what he said and the fight ensued."

"That sounds like it was about me, Roland," she responded grimly.

He'd slipped his hands into his pockets and turned toward the windows. "That depends on whether or not everything your father said was accurate. I'll check it out in the morning. For now, we should have something to eat and try to get some rest."

"I'm not hungry," she replied.

The view was breathtaking. From this window, there was at least a hundred foot drop down to the turquoise sea water. Night had fallen, and the sliver of moon cast minimal strips of light over the water. It seemed so peaceful, even in the midst of the turmoil that Val felt swirling around her.

"I know what you're feeling," Roland said as he came up behind her.

When she thought he was going to wrap his arms around her, at which time she fully intended to lean back into his embrace, he did not. Instead, he simply stood in that spot, as if letting her know that he was there if she needed him, but not overstepping in any way.

Val didn't know what she needed right then. Cora and Idelle had done exactly what they'd intended to do, upset her. Only she was certain the women wanted her to be upset over her nonexistent chances with Roland and not solely because of her father's injuries. To be perfectly honest, before they'd even arrived she'd been feeling some of what they'd intended. Even though she'd told Roland to leave, and she'd felt like that was the right thing to do, there hadn't been a day that had passed since that morning after the poker game that she had not thought about him.

She'd never envisioned herself with a prince. Ever. But Roland wasn't just a prince. In fact, there were moments when she could completely forget about his birthright and simply enjoy the man. She took a deep breath and let it out slowly.

"He's going to be alright," Roland told her. "Padget, one of the guards assisting, sent me a text that your father made it out of surgery and is resting well now. The doctors expect a full recovery."

Val nodded, happy to hear those words. It had been a bar fight. Her father had been involved in plenty of them before, but this was the first to put him in the hospital. She cupped her hands over her face and let those thoughts run through her. Then, as if something had just hit her, Val turned to face Roland.

"What do you expect, Roland?" she asked. "From me, that is. What is it that you think is going to happen between us?"

For a second, Val thought he wasn't going to answer, but then he lifted a hand and touched the strands of her hair that had been tickling her forehead. He pushed them back, his fingertips gentle against her skin.

"I think it's already happened," he told her.

She looked up into his deep chocolate-brown eyes,

trying desperately to find the trickery. She wanted to hear the slickness in his tone, to possibly thwart the smooth moves and orchestrated plans. That's what he did, wasn't it? He played women, used them for what he wanted and then tossed them back. If that were true, Val hadn't been a witness yet. Nothing he'd done for or with her in the time that she'd known him personally gave her any indication that his plan was to take her for the same ride. Nothing at all.

Still, she wondered if she should be cautious.

"All that's happened so far is sex," she replied.

He appeared hurt by her words. His head tilted slightly as if he'd been physically struck, and she thought his shoulders slumped, at least a little.

"Is that what you really think?" he asked. "Search yourself right now, Valora, and tell me if that's all you really think has happened between us."

"Roland, it's been a little over a week. Nine days, to be exact, since the night my father tried to give me to you. We've had a couple of dinners and a night of sex. Great sex, but still just sex," she said.

He nodded as if to say he heard her words, but Val didn't believe for one moment that he was going to accept what she'd just said.

"For me," Roland began, touching her cheek with the same fingers he'd fixed her hair with, "it's been like a breath of fresh air."

Val didn't know what to say.

"I told you before that you were a first. That wasn't a lie. There were moments in the past few days that I wished it were. It would be simpler that way, if this were just some conquest or something for me to do to pass the time. I guess it's unfortunate for you that its not," Roland admitted.

"I wouldn't say it's unfortunate." The words came out before she could think to stop them. Val had a sinking suspicion that might be a good thing.

"You wouldn't?" he asked and stepped closer to her. "What would you call it? What would you say is happening between us, Valora?"

"I don't know," she answered.

And that was the truth. She had no idea, at least, she didn't think she did. But her body and her mind were on different pages because before she could say another word, Val's hands were lifting to touch his arms.

She rubbed upward until they cupped his shoulders.

"I think you do," he whispered as he lowered his face to hers. "I think you know exactly what's happening."

If she did, she wasn't going to say so right now. Val was determined to leave it all behind tonight. Cora, Idelle, her father and that fight, the royal and the painter scenario, all of it was flitting away slowly but surely, from her mind as she came up on her toes and slanted her mouth over his. She was in control of this, the desire that always swept through her when she was near him. The instant punch of need that flourished when his lips were on hers. This was what was happening, every bit of this.

She was in his arms once more.

This was exactly where Roland wanted her to be. It was the reason he'd gone back to her house, even though the act contradicted everything he'd ever done in his life where women were concerned. But Roland hadn't cared. As he'd stepped out of the car and walked up to her front door, he hadn't cared one bit about any other woman he'd had the pleasure of knowing. None of them mattered. Not after Valora.

Those women and what had happened to her father had thrown his attention in a different direction, but it always came back to her. Each and every time, he was realizing, it came back to her.

He kissed her hungrily, not willing to give her any other impression at this moment other than that he wanted, no, he needed her desperately.

"I need you, V," he whispered into the line of her neck as he dragged his mouth eagerly over her skin. "I don't know why or how it happened, but it's true. I just need…you."

She held the back of his head firmly now, her own hunger showing as she pressed eagerly into him.

"I know," she gasped. "I know what you mean. That's all there is. The need."

He wanted to nod and then yell, jumping up and down because she was absolutely right. There was nothing else. No crown. No gossipers. No threats. Just them and their need for each other. That was all.

Roland pulled her dress up and over her head in seconds. He unsnapped her bra and pushed her panties down her legs. While she stepped out of her shoes, he hurriedly retrieved a condom from his wallet, then tossed the leather billfold onto the floor. His clothes immediately followed.

She grabbed the condom from him and unwrapped it. Roland was certain he'd never seen anything as sexy as the way her small hands moved over the foil wrapper. When that wrapper hit the floor he sucked in a breath. She took him in one hand, gently, rubbing her thumb over the slit of his arousal. He gritted his teeth and fought to keep his eyes from rolling back in his head. She stroked him then. From the base to his tip, she let the warmth of her hand surround his length and Roland knew he'd never felt anything as blissful in his life before. With her other hand she touched the latex to his tip and smoothed it down over him. The second she was finished, Roland was lifting her into his arms.

She wrapped her legs around his waist and he walked them to the window where he pushed her back against the glass. Behind her were the mountains and the water and space. Inside her, he thought as he pressed his length into her waiting center, was absolute peace.

He pumped instantly, in and out; he moved with the ferocity of a starved animal. Her blunt-tipped nails dug into his shoulders, her head fell back against the glass. She was breathing heavily and so was he. The sound of their bodies connecting echoed throughout the living room, spurring his desire until he wanted to simply devour her.

His hands shook as he held on to her, his body tensing all over as the pleasure simply occupied every space in his soul.

"V!" he called out to her. It was a simple letter, one syllable, one moment, one woman.

There would not be another. Roland knew that as surely as he knew the sun would always rise. He'd waited all these years, all this time to find her, and she'd been right here all along. His father had said if he'd just slow down he would be surprised to see who was standing beside him. Roland was surprised and enamored and dangerously close to falling in love.

With his arm still tight around her waist, Roland let Val's feet touch the floor. He took her mouth in another heated kiss, this time nipping her bottom lip with his teeth before sucking it into his mouth for what seemed like endless spine-tingling moments. When he finally pulled away, he turned her so that her back was now facing him. Before she could ask what was going on, he grasped her wrists and lifted her arms up over her head. When her head lolled forward, he kissed the nape of her neck. He nipped the skin along the back of her neck and across her shoulder blades. He flattened her palms on the window and continued to kiss her.

Val was breathless. She was spiraling out of control, and when she chanced opening her eyes, she saw the water below. It was fitting, she thought, because one more touch from him, one more stroke, one more word of adoration and she was going to topple right over. It would be just like free-falling off this cliff. She knew it before it even happened. She welcomed it even though she knew there would be consequences.

Then he was moving, dragging his hands down her torso until he could cup her hips. Adjusting her slightly so that her bottom was thrust in his direction, Val felt his length touch the crevice of her bottom and she groaned. He pressed right there, letting her feel the long hot length of him trying to get inside her warmth once more. She moved her hips, desperate to help him get to the spot they both wanted him to reach. When he grasped her cheeks and spread her wide, she gasped.

"Open for me," he groaned. "Please."

"Yes," she screamed. "Only for you."

Val spread her legs wider and was rewarded with the feel of his erection pressing into her in one intense motion. Her body shook with the action, her fingers slid along the glass as she attempted to grip something, anything.

"Perfect," he said when he leaned over her to lick the line of her shoulder. "This is just perfect. You. Everything."

She was shaking her head, hearing his words. Memorizing them, absorbing them into her system. He'd been saying things like this since they'd begun and it was driving her insane. If they were true, they were fabulous. If they weren't, she didn't care, she loved hearing them. Loved feeling how worked up each admission had him. She loved...

"Roland!" His name rolled off her tongue just seconds before her release took her.

She trembled all over, parts of her seeming to melt away into thin air.

"More," he said as he thrust faster and deeper into her. "Just a little more."

"Yes," she moaned. "Yes."

"Yes!" he echoed. "Yes!"

And then both their hearts were racing as he pushed into her one final time. Her body was plastered to the glass, his right behind. Their breaths fogged the window, their release filled the room with an air of satisfaction.

"You asked me what I thought was happening," she said after a minute or so of silence as they caught their breaths.

"Yeah," he said, still gasping. "You have an answer now."

Val nodded.

"It's already happened," was her easy reply.

He kissed her back and rested his forehead against hers once more. "I agree," he said. "I totally agree."

Hours later, after they'd eaten bologna sandwiches and drunk bottled orange juice, Roland and Valora lay on his bed. She was turned on her side so she could look out to the sea. He was right behind her, his body spooned against hers, his lips at her neck. In a few moments they would undoubtedly fall asleep.

"I don't want to be kept a secret," he began. "I don't want to have to sneak around with the woman I'm sleeping with, not anymore. If I'm going to be in a relationship with someone, it's going to be all-in or nothing. We're both going to work on a real and healthy relationship, or I'm not getting involved. That's what I deserve and that's all I'll accept."

Val went totally still at his words. She remembered them—it was exactly what she'd said to him that day she'd pushed him away.

He didn't ask for a reply, and because it had taken her so long to even think of one, he'd already fallen asleep. That was good, she thought, because she wasn't sure that what she was going to say was what he wanted to hear.

Actually, she wasn't sure that what she was going to

say was what either of them were ready to take on, no matter the words they'd both spoken on how totally right and magnificent this thing between them felt.

Chapter 14

Valora was in a casino.

She was wearing a maxidress with a black halter top and a black-and-white-striped skirt. The extra twenty minutes she'd taken to curl her hair had paid off, because as she walked past the mirrored wall in the front entrance, she'd caught a glimpse of the cute short style. She'd smiled and continued to walk as if there was a new and exciting destination ahead of her.

Aside from the fact that, because of her father's sickening habit she hated gambling with a passion, the casino was a fabulous place to be. At least, it was tonight.

Three days had passed since Val spent the night at Roland's cliff house. In that time, a tentative deal had been struck between Kip Sallinger, Quirio Denton and the royal family. This deal—as Val understood—was to build a new resort, complete with a golf course, spa and high-end shopping. The resort would be built on land that adjoined the spot where Mr. Sallinger's casino now sat in the town center. Roland was already working on a proposal to present to the Tourism Board and the cruise lines, selling the resort, casino and golf club combo as a package deal for tourists.

All that meant that the past three days had been filled with one dinner meeting after another. Val would work at the museum during the day, go to Roland's cliff house at night, attend a dinner meeting and then go back to Roland's cliff house for brainstorming and lovemaking until the early-morning hours. Tonight was Friday, and Val had left work an hour early because she wanted to take the extra time to not only pick out an outfit, but to make sure her hair and makeup were on point. At the dinner last night with Kris, Landry, Gary and Sam, Val had noted how together both princesses looked. She wasn't a princess, but she figured if she were going to be on Roland's arm, she should at least be presentable.

She was on Roland's arm. Going out with a prince. No matter how many times she said those things to herself, it still seemed unbelievable. As unbelievable as Tuesday afternoon, when she'd arrived at Roland's house to find a rack of clothes in his living room and shoe boxes stacked by his couch.

"Are you packing?" she'd asked.

"No," he'd replied as he came over to kiss her loudly on the lips. "I've been shopping."

He was smiling, looking quite proud of himself, and Val had felt like smiling along with him. When did such a simple thing as Roland's smile make her happy?

Maybe since Roland had secured a private suite in the hospital for her father and put out a warrant for the arrest of the man who had broken her father's arm and left his face bloody and bruised. And that wasn't all. Roland had even assured Hugo that once he was totally healed and rested, Roland would help him find a job on the island.

She was happier than she'd ever been in her whole life and she owed it all to this man.

At that realization Val had hugged Roland, pulling back after holding tight and then giving him a slow and sweet kiss.

"Wow. Is that what I get when I say I've been shopping?" he'd asked as he kept his arms locked around her waist.

Val had discovered that she loved being embraced by Roland. There was something about the way his strong arms holding her that translated to *I'll protect you, I'll cherish you*. She'd never realized how much she'd craved feeling each of those words, until now.

"No. You only have to be who you are," she'd told him.

He'd stared at her another few seconds before leaning forward and kissing the tip of her nose.

"That's the best thing anyone has ever said to me," he'd admitted.

"That should have been said to you a long time ago, Roland. You're not the man people say you are. There's so much more to you than just the title or the gambling. So much more."

"And it took you to make me see that," he'd told her.

"My father said if I stopped running I'd be surprised to see who was standing beside me. I'm glad I stopped."

"I'm glad, too," Val had told him. She was more than glad; she was proud.

And a few moments later, when Roland had told her that he'd been shopping for her all afternoon, she'd been ecstatic.

Tonight, she wore one of the dresses Roland had selected for her and she loved how she looked in it. She didn't, however, like how people looked at her when she was with Roland. They were surprised, sure, and she could go along with that. But some were talking. She should have expected it and been used to it; still, it burned to acknowledge.

"I want you to meet someone," Roland said the moment they hit the casino floor.

He was wearing a black suit with a collarless stone-gray shirt. His shoes were shined to perfection, his hair and beard groomed precisely. He looked like a movie star and Val was happy she did, too.

"Sure," she was saying as she walked beside him.

"Let me know if you want to play anything while we're here," he said, as they continued to walk over the bright red, gold and green carpet.

"No, thanks," she said and looked over to the gaming tables. "I'm totally out of my element here."

He looked over to her. "Never. You're not out of your element anywhere. But I get what you're trying to say, and listen, just because you play a game or two doesn't mean you're addicted to gambling."

She nodded because she knew what he was saying was true. But it didn't mean she was going to take that chance. From the looks of the crowd that moved along with them across the casino floor and the number of people she saw sitting at or standing around gaming tables, she was the only one who felt that way.

There were two winding staircases, one on each side of the massive casino floor. Two men dressed in black suits took the stairs ahead of Roland. He held her hand as he walked up and she followed. There were two more black-suited men behind her. His guards. She saw them a lot now. And she knew why.

Roland had confided in her that someone was taunting the royal family. He thought it had something to do with his father's impending nuptials. Roland also thought it was somehow related to the man who'd assaulted her father. For that reason, a guard now also drove behind Val wherever she went. When she was out of the car, he was at her side. It was eerie and yet eye-opening. It reminded her daily that she was dating a prince.

The entrance to another large room was roped off until Roland approached. Two women, wearing the thinnest and tightest sparkling nude-colored gowns she'd ever seen, smiled.

"Good evening, Prince Roland," they said in unison.

Roland gripped her hand even tighter, and Val wondered if he could feel the uneasiness swirling in the pit of her stomach.

He greeted the women and kept Val close as they moved through the entrance into the larger room. It was a party, from what Val could see. A four-piece ensemble in one corner was playing music, a buffet was spread against the left wall. The other side of the room was all windows so guests could enjoy the views of the mountains in the distance and the cruise ships pulling in to dock a little closer. Different-sized chandeliers sparkled from the ceiling, while high tables were covered in black cloths. Women dressed in short black shorts and tuxedo tail jackets moved throughout with trays of drinks.

"There you are," Samantha said as she walked up to them. "I was beginning to think you'd changed your mind."

"Not a chance," Roland said with a shake of his head. He leaned in to kiss his sister's cheek.

Samantha DeSaunters Montgomery beamed. She obviously loved her brother. The princess wore a long dress in a lovely shade of pink. Her long hair was pulled up in a neat bun. She looked casually pretty and aristocratic, all at the same time, while her husband stood beside her in navy blue pants and a dark gray jacket. He was an American soldier with a rugged appearance. They were a starkly different couple and yet their love was as obvious as the money floating around in this facility.

"It's good to see you again, Valora," Samantha said.

Val remembered the last time she'd seen the princess and she immediately felt embarrassed.

"Good evening, Your Highness," Val said and fell into a quick curtsy.

"You can call me Sam. There's just family around," the princess told her.

Just family, Val thought. The royal family. It was a bit to swallow, but the approach of Prince Kristian and

Princess Landry confirmed it. Val curtsied once more as she greeting the crown prince and his wife.

"You look lovely," Landry said, after telling Val she preferred to be called by her first name only.

She was American, too, and had only been a princess for a few months. Val liked each of these women.

"Thank you," Val replied.

That was truly a compliment coming from a woman who was known for her fashion sense.

"Did you like the other outfits?" Landry asked Val after they were all served a drink.

Val immediately looked to Roland, who shrugged as he took a sip from his glass. "I said I was shopping. I didn't say I did it alone," he replied to her questioning gaze.

"I loved it all," Val said after shaking her head at him. "Thank you so much for taking the time to select those items for me."

She didn't know if she should be embarrassed that another woman had to choose the right clothes for her to wear while she was with Roland, or just thankful that she'd received a new wardrobe for being with a guy she was crazy about. The latter won, and Val relaxed as Landry waved away her comment.

"It was no problem. I enjoy what I do. With the magazine launch and the big fashion show coming up next month, I don't get a lot of time to simply style like I used to. When Roland called me and told me what he wanted, I hopped on the chance to help."

So, Roland had called his sister-in-law and told her about Val. She wondered what that conversation had entailed.

"I really appreciate it. I had no idea Roland was going to do something like that," Val said.

The guys had huddled around Roland as if they were protecting him after his shopping comment, and the women had come closer to Val.

"We didn't either," Sam said. "I mean, I'll admit that I kind of thought there was something big between you two."

"How?" Val asked. "I mean, there wasn't at first, and then there was. But I didn't tell anyone anything. I wasn't trying to get any attention. It just happened."

Sam touched a hand to Val's shoulder. "Stop. It's okay. I know you weren't gunning for him. If you were, you wouldn't be standing here today."

Val must have looked confused by Sam's words because the princess continued to smile as she nodded.

"I know my brother, and if he thought you were disingenuous about being with him or plotting something bigger, he would have dismissed you instantly. That's just how he is," Sam said.

"I haven't known him as long as she has, but Sam's right. Roland does not play games," Landry added.

Val sighed with relief. "I just don't want other people to think this was all some master plan."

"You can stop that right now," Sam told her.

"Stop what?" Val asked.

"Giving a damn what other people think," Landry explained. "No matter what you do or say, they're always going to form their own opinion. They're entitled to it. You, on the other hand, don't have to hear their opinions or take them to heart."

When Val only looked from one of them to the other, Sam shrugged and said, "She's right."

Val grinned and relaxed. "I really like you two," she said and took a sip of the drink that had been handed to her a few moments ago.

A few minutes passed in a conversation about them having dinner and taking in a show, then the guys were back, this time with someone in tow.

"Quirio Denton, I would like for you to meet—" Kristian's words were cut short as the tall, slim man who had come over with the men spoke.

"The royal women," he said, stepping forward and bowing before the three of them.

"Princess Samantha," Quirio said when he stood straight. "It is a pleasure to meet you in person. I have been a fan of yours for quite some time."

The man was smooth. Val would give him that. He was over six feet tall with a dark chocolate complexion and bald head. He wore all white, pants, shirt, jacket and shoes. There was a huge gold watch at his wrist and a large sparkling diamond in his left ear.

"It is nice to meet you, Mr. Denton. I've heard a lot about you in the past few weeks," Sam said, while allowing him to take her hand and kiss the back of it.

Gary had returned to stand next to his wife, giving Denton a look that clearly said he would break the much slimmer man in two if he took the cordial kiss too far.

"And the newest princess, the lovely American who stumbled across her Prince Charming and snagged the aloof Prince Kristian." Denton easily lifted Landry's hand kissed its back, as well.

Landry smiled in return. "It is a pleasure to meet you, Mr. Denton."

"And this is…" Denton began when he finally stood directly in front of Val.

"I'm Va—" Val began to say, but she was cut off by Roland, who had come to stand right beside her, taking both her hands in his.

"This is Valora Harrington. She's with me and there will be no kissing of her hand, you rake," Roland said before chuckling at Denton.

Denton joined him in laughing as he continued to stare at Val. "Okay, I see, Your Highness. No need to explain further."

Denton had been about to turn away, but he stopped and looked back at Val. She'd been shaking her head at Roland, but they both stopped when Denton yelled, "I know you!"

Val startled and the hand Roland held of hers began to shake. Did her father owe this man money too? How else would he know her?

"Excuse me?" Roland asked as he took a defensive step in front of Val.

Denton grinned, straight white teeth showing with his action. He pointed beyond Roland to Val and said again, "I know her!"

"How exactly do you know her?" Gary asked, suspicion clear in his voice.

They'd circled around her, Kristian and Landry, Gary and Sam. Both couples had come to Val's side while Roland stood in front of her. With the quick motion of the royal family, the guards who had been hanging back at a safe distance also moved forward.

"My Moonlight," Denton said. *"An Island Morning."*

Val relaxed enough to give a small smile. "You know my work?"

Denton nodded. "I own those two pieces," he told her. "I wanted to purchase more, but the manager at the museum here said there were no more."

"She doesn't sign her work," Roland stated, his tone still leery.

"No. No she does not," Denton said. "But once you purchase the painting, you get a certificate of authenticity. It has the artist's name on it."

"He's right," Val replied.

They were the first two paintings she'd sold. Eddie, the manager of the museum, hadn't wanted to include them in the Homegrown wing of the museum where they showcased all forms of art from citizens of the island. He'd said it was a conflict since Val worked there, and he didn't want anyone to think he was showing favoritism. So he'd put the paintings in the gift shop, instead. Val had been sure nobody would ever see them in there, with the quantity of other items on display in that store. But this man had.

"I didn't know you were a painter," Sam said immediately. "There's no exhibit at the museum under your name. If there was, I would know. All new exhibits have to be approved by a member of the royal family, which usually means me."

Val cleared her throat. Everyone was staring at her, but she was used to that. "My manager thought it would be a conflict if he featured my paintings since I work there."

Denton nodded. "Ahhh, I was wondering why such

good pieces were in the gift shop. They were on the floor behind a stack of watercolors, at that. I knew immediately what they were worth."

"What were they worth?" Val asked, because to date she had not been informed that any of her paintings had been sold.

"Well, I would think you would have been satisfied with your commission," Denton said to her.

Val was face went blank.

"You didn't know your pictures had been sold?" Roland asked.

"No," she replied shaking her head.

"Well," Gary said, "I believe that means someone will be getting fired first thing tomorrow morning."

"Fired and possibly arrested," Kristian added.

"They're signaling us over there," Landry stated. "I think they're ready for us."

Val breathed a sigh of relief because she didn't like the way Roland was looking at Denton. She especially didn't like learning that she'd sold two paintings but hadn't received any money. She was placing a call to Eddie the moment she left the party.

"That's the good thing about this tropical climate," Denton was saying, moments later when they were all seated at the table. "We can break ground as soon as next month. Give my team a few weeks to get some plans drawn up and approved. I've got a construction crew ready to go at a moment's notice."

"The height of cruise season will be starting toward the end of April and it'll run straight through to end of September," Kip added.

"We're leaving for the States right after the fashion show in January," Sam stated. "Gary needs time to work on his book and I have to begin working with the hospital there on our plans for the children's foundation. If you can assure me that we'll have final plans by the first of the year, I can work on scheduling meetings with the cruise lines around that time."

This little get-together had been Roland's idea, yet he was sitting at the table thinking of all the things he planned to say to Eddie Bishop, the manager of the museum. Firing the man wasn't going to be enough. After seeing Val's paintings, he'd also wondered why they weren't featured at the museum. He'd planned to address that issue, but hadn't gotten around to it yet. At this point, it was going to be a priority.

Now, however, he needed to get this deal with the casino and the new resort completed.

"I'll join you for those meetings," he said.

Sam arched a brow in response. "Really? Then I'll be sure to run the proposed dates by you ahead of time. I wouldn't want to hinder any of your travel plans."

"I don't have any travel plans," Roland said to his sister. "At least, not until after Christmas. Then I was thinking Valora might like to go skiing in the Alps."

Val clearly hadn't expected him to say that, as evidenced by the way she immediately looked at him. Roland grinned at her. He'd never imagined he would love surprising a woman as much as he did Valora. In the past few days he'd realized how much he loved being with her.

"That sounds like a wonderful idea," Denton commented. "I have a château in Switzerland. Consider it yours for however long you wish to stay."

"I'm sure that's going to be lovely," Sam said.

"Thank you very much," Valora said to Denton. "That's very generous of you."

The man took that as an opening and he reached over to take Valora's hand. When he'd insisted on sitting next to her, Roland had sent him another warning glare. Now, it seemed, his scowls weren't going to be enough.

"What you can do for me in return is simple," Denton told Valora.

"Careful, Denton, this deal isn't done yet," Roland said, not liking the punch of jealousy that so easily coursed through him.

The guy answered Roland by tossing his head back and laughing. "As we say in America, you've got this guy sprung," he told Valora.

Landry laughed, and Roland was afraid Gary might have, too, if he hadn't excused himself to take a phone call a few minutes ago.

"Just tread lightly and say what you have to say so you can let her hand go," Roland told the man with a shake of his head.

He knew the phrase *sprung* very well, even if he wasn't American. It had never occurred to him that he would ever be in that position, but evaluating the meaning—basically that he'd fallen pretty hard for her—he admitted to himself that it wasn't far from the truth.

"You have no worries, Prince Roland. I never pursue what is already taken," Denton said. "Besides, what I am asking for is something that I think will be beneficial to all of us."

"What's that?" Valora asked.

She'd flushed when Roland had spoken to Denton, but he was more concerned with making sure Denton knew Roland wasn't going to tolerate any form of flirtation. He'd apologize for making her uncomfortable later.

"I want to commission your paintings," Denton told her. "We can feature them in the resort. What better way to sell the resort and this island than to have fabulous artwork by one of Grand Serenity's own?"

"That's actually a wonderful idea," Kris said.

"It's a fabulous idea," Sam told them. "I wish I'd come up with it."

"How many paintings do you have?" Landry asked. "I would love to see them."

Valora shook her head. "Not nearly enough to fill a resort."

"We won't be ready to open until probably late next year. That'll give you time to paint away," Denton told her.

"I have to work," she was saying, and Roland thought she sounded a little overwhelmed.

"Nonsense, if you're commissioned to do all the artwork for the resort, you won't need that job at the museum anymore," Denton told her.

"Not work at the museum?" Valora asked. "I love the museum."

"Maybe you can do both," Roland stated. "A few hours a week at the museum and then spend the rest of your time painting. You're extremely talented, Valora. There's no reason that your work shouldn't be shared with the world. We can get you an agent to work on

Denton's contract with you. If that's what you want to do."

"Wow," Valora said. "I had no idea that coming here tonight would end in an offer like this. I'd like a couple of days to let this all sink in, if it's okay with you."

Denton nodded. "I'll wait until you're ready," he told her. I really think your pictures will be great for the resort. We can plan architecture and interior design based around your ideas for the paintings. But I'll let you take a few days, though. Prince Roland knows how to reach me," Denton said.

Roland nodded. He said something about having Denton's cell phone number and email just as Gary returned to the table. As if the way he was looking at them didn't say something was wrong, the way he walked directly to Sam and pulled her chair from the table, announcing they were leaving, said it all.

"What happened?" Roland asked.

"Amari Taylor's been sighted," Gary said. "We're all leaving. Now."

Kristian was already pushing away from the table and standing. Roland followed, noting their guards had all moved closer. Roland reached for Valora, who was already standing. She put her hand in his without question and they hastily moved from the room.

It wasn't until they were all in one of the service elevators heading down to the first floor of the casino that Gary elaborated.

"He was here," he said grimly. "He walked right into the casino and took a seat at the craps table. One of the guards saw him and called the base for verification on how Amari looked. That's when they called me, right after they confirmed it was him."

"Did they catch him?" Sam asked.

Gary shook his head.

"Amari must have known they were onto him. He headed to a back door. Two guards followed him out and called to the parking lot for the guards out there to come in and back them up. By the time the backup arrived, the two who'd made the original sighting were bleeding in the back alley," Gary told them.

"Oh, my..." Landry said and then stopped herself. "He's out of control."

"And that's precisely what's going to get him caught," Gary said when they arrived on the first floor and the guards led them down a dark hallway.

"He should have never come back to Grand Serenity. The fact that he did says this is personal for him. And personal means emotions are attached. Those emotions are going to be the end of him."

By the time Gary finished, they were outside. Three white Mercedes sedans pulled up, a guard immediately jumping from each car and opening the back door for them to get in.

"To the palace," Gary announced. "It's easier to keep everyone safe if we're all under the same roof."

Roland knew he was talking to him, and while he preferred his cliff house, he also recognized the logic behind his brother-in-law's direction. He nodded at Gary and began leading Valora to a car. He paused and yelled back to Gary who was still standing outside after he'd already put Sam in the car. He was watching to make sure the princes were safe in their vehicles before he got into his.

"Send someone for Hugo Harrington," Roland said to Gary. "Amari might go after him again, now that I'm sure he knows things have changed between me and Valora."

Gary nodded. "You're right. I'll make a call as soon as I get in the car."

Roland nodded and slipped inside. He fastened his seat belt and then reached out to take Valora's hand again.

"Is this guy ever going to stop coming after you and your family?" Valora asked him when their driver pulled away.

"Not until we stop him," Roland replied.

Chapter 15

Val watched as the staff set the table for breakfast. She was early, she knew, but Roland had left the bedroom a while ago, right after receiving a text message from Gary. Today was the day and she was anxious for it to begin. This would be the first royal wedding that she'd ever attended. It was going to be magical, even if the royal siblings despised the woman their father was marrying. As for Val, she didn't despise Malayka Sampson, but she wasn't overly fond of the woman, either. Still, it was Malayka's wedding day.

Across the entire island everyone was eager to see snippets of this event on their televisions from the only one of the local reporters who was allowed access. Val had seen the woman last night at the rehearsal dinner. She'd been hastily taking notes while her cameraman walked around with one of the men Val had learned that Malayka hired to help supervise the event. This day was going to be huge and Val was excited to have an up close and personal spot to enjoy.

The last week and a half had practically flown by with the palace abuzz with preparations. As for Val, working on sketches and going to the museum for the four tours a week she'd agreed to work, had been taking up most of her time. When she wasn't working she was with Roland, and when he was working she would sit at the pool and chat with Landry and/or Sam.

It was funny how easily she'd slipped into the routine of staying at the palace. While she knew it was for her safety, and a part of her had entertained the idea that it might be too early in their relationship for her and Roland to live together, she was enjoying herself immensely. Even if there was a madman on the loose and guards flanking them every moment of the day.

There had been moments when Val thought this was all a dream. The quick twists and turns her life had taken in the past month seemed to be something straight out of a script. For the fun of it, she pinched herself and chuckled at the jolt of pain.

"Torturing yourself," her father said.

She hadn't heard him come up behind her and hadn't expected to see him there. Val had thanked Roland for thinking of her father and bringing him to stay at the palace, as well. She was sure it wasn't just for Hugo's safety. Roland knew that all her father had ever wanted was what he foolishly thought was his rightful place in the royal family. If that meant he could stay there for a few weeks, or until they caught this Amari Taylor character, she would be forever grateful to Roland for giving him that.

"No, Dad," she replied. "Just assuring myself that this is really happening."

"Yes," Hugo told her. "It really is. Rafe's marrying that crazy gal for sure."

Val shook her head. "Look how beautiful everything is. The crystal is shining, the silver sparkling. The entire palace is full of flowers. And the ballroom." She clapped a hand to her chest. "Did you see the ballroom? I snuck a peek in there before heading down here for breakfast. It's absolutely stunning."

Malayka had gone all out with the elegant gold theme. There was sheer netting hanging from the gold ceiling. Tables were covered in champagne-colored cloths and there were gold chairs. Tall gold candelabra on each table had white candles ready to be lit. White roses were everywhere, spilling from massive gold vases, nestled in corners in crystal containers, strewn across each table. It smelled as wonderful as it looked, all of which made Val even more excited to slip into the gown Landry had declared was perfect for her to wear today.

"He's making a big mistake, if you ask me," Hugo continued.

"That's probably why they didn't ask you, Dad," Val said as she leaned against the doorjamb, waiting for the others to join them at the family breakfast.

This was the main dining room where Val had learned that the family took most of their meals. There was a long cherrywood table here; today it was covered with a lace tablecloth. The plates they were using were gold rimmed, and the centerpiece was composed of more roses, just like the ones in the ballroom. Early morning sunlight poured in through the large window behind the head of the table where Prince Rafferty usually sat. It was a perfect day, she thought. And the food smelled pretty terrific, too.

"Smells like French toast," Val said to her father.

He chuckled. "That's still your favorite breakfast food, after all this time."

She'd nodded, glad to take her father's mind off the mistake he thought Prince Rafe was making. For the next fifteen minutes her father talked about all the food he'd enjoyed during his stay at the palace. Val only half listened. She was much more intrigued by the sound of pure pleasure she heard in his voice. It was the first time she'd heard him sound this way and she found that she really liked it.

The next sound, however, Val was sure she never wanted to hear again.

It was like nothing she'd ever heard before, a loud crushing sound followed by what she thought might be gunshots.

"What the hell is that?" Hugo yelled as he moved closer to Val.

"I don't know," she said, as one of the staff members came running into the dining room.

"It's another bomb!" the woman yelled.

"Oh, my word!" Hugo exclaimed. "Come on! We've got to get out of here!"

He was pulling Val out of the room and down the hallway before she had a moment to say anything. There were other people running, but Val looked for

him, anyway. She didn't want to leave without Roland.
Screams came next, along with more footsteps. These
were louder and moved quicker. She and Hugo had just
reached one of the side doors of the palace when three
uniformed officers pushed past them.

Hugo kept them moving until they were out on the
lawn. That's when Val finally stopped, yanking her
hand away from her father's.

"Where's Roland? Where's the family?" she asked.

"I don't know and we aren't sticking around to find
out. It's taking them too damn long to catch him. Looks
like he's still going on with his plan," Hugo insisted.

"What do you know about a plan?" Val asked him.

"Never mind," he said. "Let's just keep going."

They were moving around to the front of the palace
by then, her father out of breath and Val still anxiously
looking around. When she caught sight of Landry she
ran in her direction, tugging her father's arm and telling him to follow her. He did, and they came to where
Landry was standing, four guards around her.

"What's going on?" Val asked.

Landry was shaking her head. "They want to get us
to safety," she said. "There's been some type of threat."

"Threat?" Hugo asked. "You didn't hear that bang-
ing? Whatever they were threatening to do, they've
done!"

"No," Landry told him. "Kris called me just a few
moments ago. He said they received a tip that Amari
had hired a guy to crash through the gates with explosives in his truck. They wanted to stop the wedding
once and for all."

Val shivered at the thought. "Roland?"

Landry touched a hand to her shoulder. "He's safe. He was with Kris and Gary. The truck was already on its way by the time they received the tip. They barely had enough time to get the guards set up at the gate. They planned to shoot the driver and stop the truck from getting close to the palace. But I'm not sure that worked."

"Let's get you a better distance away, just in case," one of the guards said to Landry.

They ran down an incline toward a smaller building. The guards escorted them inside.

"Now what?" Hugo asked.

"We wait," Landry said.

"Wait for what? To be killed?" Hugo continued.

"No," Val whispered. "Please, no."

The message had been clear. The plan was for the truck to ride onto the property and for the driver to detonate enough explosives to wipe out the entire palace.

Gary had sent text messages to Kris, Roland and Rafe the minute he'd received the call. The four of them had quickly come up with a plan. That plan had worked, partially.

The truck driver hadn't heeded the warnings of the guards or the police officers and, instead, had tried to break through the front. It was at that point the guards opened fire, killing the driver just as the truck slammed into the gate. Grand Serenity's scaled-down version of a bomb squad had been dispatched while Gary briefed Roland and the others. They were just arriving when the truck made contact. The officers were immediately assessing the explosives that were in the back of the truck.

"It wasn't Amari," Gary told them when he came back to the room in the separate building where the new security team was housed. That's where he'd told Roland, Kris and Rafe they would be safest.

"What do you mean it wasn't him?" Roland asked. "Who else would it be?"

"Just as the message said, he hired someone," Gary told them.

"So, where's Amari?" Kris asked.

"He's here," Rafe replied this time. His tone deep and somber. "If it's personal for this guy, he would want to be close by to see our demise."

Gary nodded. "That's why I have the guards searching the palace. Everyone has been evacuated until the search is complete.

"Not everyone," Kris said from where he stood at a window. "Look!"

"I thought you sent guards to get her and Sam!" Rafe yelled before going to the door and opening it. He was running out before anyone could stop him, so they all followed him, instead.

A short distance away, Malayka was running toward a group of police officers. She was stopped before she could get to them when a man came up from behind and grabbed her, slamming her to the ground. At the same time, Sam came out of the house with two guards at her side. When she saw her family, she ran over.

Rafe was enraged as he tried to get to Malayka. Roland passed his father, so he came up on them first.

"You stupid bitch! You wouldn't have any of this if it weren't for me!" The guy was yelling as he reached down to grab Malayka by the hair.

Roland punched him. Then, when the man released Malayka and stumbled back, Roland punched him again. The second blow was because he had a pretty good idea who this was.

"If I go down, you go down! I told you that from the start! Don't think you're gonna live in splendor while I rot! You're nothing but a trifling slut, just like your mother was!"

That earned him another punch, this time from Kris. Rafe was helping Malayka up off the ground when Gary finally came around to the guy to slap cuffs on his wrists.

"Amari Taylor, I presume," Gary said.

"My name is Amari Vansig. And she's not in love with you," Amari told Rafe. "She's been using you all along."

"Liar!" Malayka yelled and lunged at him. "You're a filthy liar!"

"And you're a greedy bitch!" Amari shot back.

"Get him the hell out of here," Rafe said as he pulled Malayka away from the man.

Gary nodded to two of the guards, waiting until they came and escorted Amari away.

"What are we going to do with her?" Kris asked.

"If he's right, and she was in on this with him, then she can go where he's going," Gary said.

Roland and Kris nodded their agreement.

But Rafe stood perfectly still. He stared at Malayka and made one simple statement. "Tell me the truth."

For an instant, Roland thought she might actually insult them all. Instead, she took a step back from where Rafe stood and shook her head.

"I messed up everything," she began with tears streaming down her face. "The plan was for me to seduce you. To get into the palace and find something, anything to blackmail you with."

"Why?" was Rafe's immediate question. "What did I do to you or him that made you want this revenge against me and mine?"

Roland recognized the seething anger that lay like a thin sheet over the hurt within his father. He knew because he'd felt it himself when he'd learned that his mother was dead.

Malayka didn't even bother to wipe her face. The woman who once made sure she was perfectly primped at all times was standing in the center of the palace's courtyard wearing a white silk robe and missing one fluffy-toed slipper. There was a rip on one arm of the robe and the corner of her mouth was bleeding.

"He was our grandfather," she answered quietly.

"Who was?" Rafe asked.

"He wasn't lying about that part at least. His real name is Amari Marco Vansig. Marco Vansig was our grandfather," Malayka told Rafe.

Roland heard Kris curse and knew his brother's mind had clicked at the same time Roland's had. They thought of the accounts at the bank. The ones that were opened under the name A. M. Vansig. Roland had also discovered they were funded with money embezzled from two of the world's richest Americans. One of them had employed Malayka and the other had been engaged to her.

They'd only connected all these dots late last night and had planned to speak to Rafe this morning before the breakfast. But Gary's text message had come first.

Years ago, Malayka had gone by the name Malinda Sampson, and neither of the billionaires had wanted the scandal that would have been attached to trying to prosecute the much-younger woman who had slept with and stolen from them.

"Amari's mother mother was Amabelle Vansig. She was Marco Vansig's oldest daughter."

"His only child," Rafe stated coldly. "Marco Vansig had a daughter who would have never been able to carry on as ruler of this island. Their family would have instantly lost control upon his death."

"The death that your father caused," she replied. "If Josef DeSaunters had not led that revolt against the ruling government, Marco Vansig would have lived longer and Amabelle would have been married. Her future would have been secured."

"He was selling her to the vicious ruler of a Mediterranean island whom he owed a large sum of money to," Rafe stated evenly. "She would have likely been beaten and abused like the man's previous wives. Is that what Amari would have called a secure future?"

From what Roland had read about the man who had once ruled Grand Serenity, he wasn't at all surprised to be hearing about this wedding agreement for the first time. Actually, for a moment, it reminded him of Hugo Harrington and all his shenanigans to get Valora married into royalty. In that moment he felt very sad for Hugo, but extremely relieved that he and Valora had found their own happiness in their own time.

"She would have married and they would have had money. Amari would not have been born in shame and filth. His mother would not have turned into a vicious drunk, abusing him every day until he grew taller and stronger than her and whichever man she was entertaining at the time. He got away from Amabelle and her boyfriend and the run-down house in the Bahamas where Amabelle had been forced to live, escaping to the United States. He did not hear from or see his mother again until he heard she'd killed herself a year ago."

Rafe stared at her without moving. He stood no more than four feet away from her, but he did not make any move to go to her, to touch her or to console her, even as her shoulders jerked and she cried a little harder.

"When did you meet him?" Roland heard his father ask. "When did you hook up with Vansig's grandson and plan this revenge?"

His voice was stern and cold, distant and serious. He was in full Prince of Grand Serenity mode now. There was nothing personal here, nothing except for the twitch in his father's jaw that said his patience was wearing very thin.

Malayka wrapped her arms around her chest then, shaking as she took another breath. She appeared to be cold—in addition to upset—as if the chill from Rafe's reaction to her was a physical one.

"Two years ago," she said, shaking her head so that the strands of hair that had fallen into her face moved slightly. "I was in New York at Fashion Week. I had front-row seats because I was dating one of the designers then," she continued.

Roland almost offered the fact that she was engaged to the man and had managed to siphon a couple of million dollars from an account he had unwisely added her name to.

"We met backstage. He'd made a name for himself in the States as a hairstylist to the stars. After seeing him work on a few of the models, I thought he was definitely talented, but kind of sad. He thought I was available. Luckily there were bodyguards all around me throughout the show."

"Lucky because you did not want to be available to a man with a smaller bank account?" Rafe asked.

Roland probably wouldn't have phrased that question so kindly. After a quick glance at Kris and Gary he figured they were thinking the same thing. As for Sam, her arms were also folded across her chest, but the look on her face as she glared at Malayka spoke of nothing but anger and contempt.

"No," Malayka said, then gave a wry chuckle. "Lucky because when we met up another year later, after my breakup with the designer and just after Amari found out his mother was dead, we discovered we actually had a lot in common. He mentioned Grand Serenity Island and I told him that my mother had been born here. We were both shocked to learn that we shared the same grandfather."

"Marco Vansig had one child," Rafe insisted.

Her arms fell to her sides as she took a step forward. The guards who had been standing right behind Roland, Kris and Sam moved in. Rafe lifted a hand to stop them.

Malayka ignored everyone but Rafe.

"He had one legal child and one illegitimate one. I was fortunate enough to be the daughter of Cessaly Sincero. She was sixteen when Marco Vansig raped her. I was the product of that encounter."

Roland wanted to shake her right at that very moment. While he and his siblings had thought all along that Malayka was up to no good. They'd had no idea how deep the treachery ran.

"So, you two believed you were the ultimate losers of a war you had no part in and decided to plan your revenge," Rafe said. "You lied to me day after day, and then you tried to kill me, to kill my children."

The prince's body shook with rage now.

"No," she said and moved to him again. This time she reached out and touched his father's arm.

Rafe did not move a muscle. He did not even look down at her.

Sam, however, had stepped closer to their father, the look on her face and her stance clearly sending the message that she was more than ready to do bodily harm to Malayka.

"I was only supposed to find information to blackmail you. I thought I could use the bank accounts, so I broke into Kris's office in search of a paper trail of the deposits into the account. Then it dawned on me that the money would be traced back to the men I'd embezzled it from. Amari wanted to rule Grand Serenity. He wanted to shame you and your family out of the palace. That's all."

"No, that was not all." Sam spoke up then. "You tried to have my father's car run off the road. A bomb went off in our house when hundreds of people were here as our guests. Somebody shot at me…and you, for that matter! And we would all be dead or severely injured right at this moment if the extra security we were forced to hire hadn't caught the man you paid to drive through the gates with a truck full of explosives!"

Gary moved in at that point, taking Sam's arm and pulling her closer to him. She'd begun to cry, she was so upset. Roland clenched his teeth at the helplessness he felt at this moment.

Amari had already been carried away. He would be on his way to the jail again, this time to be chained to his bed in a cell until the trial. Malayka was still here, still inflicting pain on his family and Roland desperately wanted it to stop.

"I couldn't find anything," Malayka continued, pulling on Rafe's shirt in an attempt to get him to look at her.

It didn't work.

"There was nothing to find, Rafe. You are a man of integrity. Your family, even him," she added with a roll of her eyes in Roland's direction, "manage to live and to rule by the same strong principles and standards that your father had. I looked and I looked. I listened in on conversations, went through personal papers in your office. I even hired Landry, thinking that maybe she could seduce Roland and get some type of scandal going. But it didn't work. Everything started to backfire," she said. "You asked me to marry you and it felt so real, Rafe. Everything we shared began to feel so real. I was planning a royal wedding. I was going to be a princess. Finally."

"But Vansig wanted to rule," Kris interjected. "He wanted to bring Grand Serenity back into the Vansig family. You messed up the plan."

"Yes," Malayka answered, but did not look at Kris when she did.

Instead, she lowered her head until her face touched the sleeve of Rafe's shirt.

"Yes, I messed up because I fell in love. For the first time in my life, I'm in love."

"Lying bitch!" Sam yelled in her direction.

Malayka only shook her head as she looked up to Rafe. "I've lied about many things in my life, but not this. That's why Rafe wasn't in the car that day. I waited until I knew that the driver was scheduled to bring him back to the palace to call Rafe and tell him that the mine owner had called for him on his personal line at the palace. I knew Rafe would go to see him while he was close to the man's house. I knew he would not be in that car."

They all stilled at her words.

"The reason the bomb didn't kill everyone in the ballroom was because I moved it. They had planted it under one of the buffet tables. It would have killed everyone in the ballroom."

"Including you," Rafe said through clenched teeth.

"The day before that, I had told Amari I couldn't do this anymore. I told him I was in love with you and that I wanted to marry you. I tried to convince him that I would keep him as my personal stylist and I would pay him lots of money so he could live in the palace, in the lifestyle he insisted was his birthright. I thought that was a good deal for both of us. We were Vansigs and we were back in the palace, after all."

She shook her head then.

"He was so angry. If you hadn't found that construction worker and eventually arrested Amari, I don't know what he would have done next."

"How about hire another guy to shoot at my sister and then escape from jail?" Roland finished for her.

"I didn't know he was going to do any of that. Later that day I got an email from him," she told them.

"The email that we intercepted," Gary said.

"We had a plan and I felt bad about not holding up my part of the bargain. But I loved you, Rafe. I loved you and I wanted to marry you. I even followed that creep Morty Javis to Sam's office the night of the Founder's Day Ball. I'd overheard some of his conversations with and about Sam. I knew his type, and I figured he was going to make a move. I tried to help her."

They were all silent, then, because that part of her story rang true. Morty had attacked both Malayka and Sam in her office that night. They'd all wondered why Malayka was there in the first place, but the fact that Gary had killed Morty seemed to overshadow that question.

"I know that all of you have been against me. Rafe, I told you they weren't going to like me and you were the one who insisted that they would get used to it, that we were going to be together, regardless," she said, both her hands now on Rafe's chest, her imploring gaze staring up at him.

Roland, and he suspected everyone who was standing there at the moment, waited for Rafe's reaction. Malayka had just admitted to being in on the plot that had almost killed members of this family. Sure, she was now declaring her love for Rafe, but wasn't it too late for that? In Roland's mind, yes. There was no question. She could not love Rafe and knowingly sit by while his family was targeted. Even if she didn't carry out any of those heinous acts herself, she'd known who was behind them and she did nothing to stop him.

Rafe moved slowly, lifting his hands to grasp Malayka's wrists and push her away from him. She looked stricken when he immediately released his hold on her and took a few steps back.

"You forget that I know what it is to be in love with someone," he told her. "There was never a moment that I did not trust Vivienne with my life and with the lives of our children. No matter what I may have thought I felt for you, the trust is gone," he said somberly.

"Rafe—" she began, but Rafe only shook his head.

It was a quick and definite motion, one that had Malayka's lips snapping immediately shut.

"If you loved me, you would have never set out to trick me or to harm my family. When you knew they were being targeted, you should have come forward. You should have told me or the police. You should have done something."

"I did. I tried to stop him," Malayka insisted.

"On your own terms," Rafe continued. "You tried to stop him without implicating your part in the plan. When you love someone their welfare, their happiness takes priority."

"What about my happiness?" Malayka yelled back at him. "What about my welfare? My mother was thrown out of her family home when they found out she was carrying Vansig's child! I grew up on the streets when I should have been given more regard. I should have been somebody!"

"That may be true," Rafe told her. "But you will never be my wife."

After the words were spoken, Rafe turned away from her. He looked to Gary and gave him a nod.

"I want them prosecuted to the fullest extent of the law," Rafe said and continued walking until he disappeared inside the house.

Gary motioned to the two guards, who immediately moved to where Malayka stood. One of them grabbed her from each side and walked her away. To her credit, she didn't say another word. She didn't make another plea. She simply walked out of their lives almost as mysteriously as she had come to be there in the first place.

Fifteen minutes later, Roland, Kris, Sam and Gary walked back into the palace. Police were still moving about the property, even though the threat of any bombs or other explosives had been cleared. Huge fresh flower arrangements that had been brought in for the wedding created a fragrant atmosphere in the front foyer. Roland was surprised to see Landry and Valora also there.

"Is everything alright?" Landry went straight to Kris.

Valora came to stand beside Roland. "I can leave if you want me to," she said quietly to him.

"Nonsense," he said with a shake of his head as he took her hand. "You're father knows as much, if not more about this family than I do. That makes you one of us."

"For better or for worse," Sam said glumly. "Malayka admitted to her part in this debacle."

"Oh, no," Landry said as Kris wrapped an arm around her. "I didn't want it to be true. I mean, I didn't like Malayka, I know that none of you did, but for your father's sake, I wanted her to be genuine."

"She was," Sam said. "A genuine liar. Her and her so-called cousin Amari. They both deserve every bit of whatever the courts decide to give them."

Kris shook his head when Landry looked up at him in question. "I'll tell you the whole sordid story later. Now, I think we all need a drink or a nap or something."

"I can get on board with a drink," Gary replied.

Roland shook his head. "I can't believe this is how this day has turned out."

"Me, either," Rafe said, surprising each of them by entering the foyer, now dressed in his tuxedo.

"Where are you going, Daddy?" Sam asked him.

"Well," Rafe began as he came to a stop in front of his family. "I was thinking that we have all this food and entertainment planned for tonight. Somebody should just get married."

In that instant, all eyes moved from Rafe with no subtlety at all to Roland and Valora.

"What?" Roland asked.

"You love her, don't you?" Rafe asked his son.

Roland looked his father straight in the eye and declared, "Yes, Dad. I love her."

Rafe smiled and nodded. "Then you should marry her, son. Tomorrow is promised to no man."

"He's right," Landry chimed in. "For the last eight months we've all been walking around, either planning or dreading—or possibly a little of both—this day. Just because one wedding won't take place, doesn't mean there shouldn't be any nuptials exchanged today."

Rafe began to laugh. "You picked a good one, Kris. A mighty good and smart one."

"I stood still for forty-five minutes getting fitted for that tux," Gary added. "I guess I might as well get the chance to wear it."

Roland saw them all looking at him expectantly. He felt Valora standing at his side, but she hadn't said a word. He was almost afraid to look over at her. Had he planned on marrying her? Of course he did. He loved her. It was the obvious next step. Obvious to everyone including him, he supposed. But was this how he wanted to do it? Was this how she wanted to get married? In a couple of hours, with plans that had been made by someone else, for someone else?

He began to smile as he realized that this was perfect. It was as unpredicted and surprising as their love.

"Will you do it?" he asked when he finally turned to look at her.

She was smiling at him in return, her eyes bright with excitement. "Will I do what?"

Sam snickered and Landry covered her mouth to keep everyone from knowing that she was doing the same. Okay, Roland thought, if they wanted it that way...

He moved to stand directly in front of Valora and slowly went down on one knee.

Behind him Roland could hear Hugo clapping.

Roland took Valora's hand and kissed its back. He looked up to her and asked with the most sincerity he'd ever felt in his life, "Will you marry me? Today?"

She laughed then and shook her head. "This is insane. They said you would never marry. They said I would never marry a prince."

"They're not us," Roland told her. "This is just you and me. Tell me you'll be my wife…in about three hours."

"Yes," she said still shaking her head. "Yes. Yes. Yes!"

Sam added to Hugo's clapping and Landry gave a loud "Yay."

"Well, then, yes, let's do it!" Roland exclaimed.

Epilogue

The third royal wedding.

Valora had not planned one part of this wedding. If she had, she would have selected different flowers—being sure to include her mother's angel wing begonias—and different table centerpieces. She would have chosen a local musician to play that love song her father used to sing to her as the music she would walk down the aisle to.

Her dress would have been vintage, straight fitting and simple. She would have grown her hair out so that it could be put up in some naturally casual style. And it would have been by the sea, so that as she said her vows she could hear the rolling waves and smell the fresh sea air.

This, no matter how beautiful, was not her dream.

Instead, it was her reality.

Today was her wedding day, Val thought as she walked down the aisle arm-in-arm with her very excited and proud father in the ballroom just three hours after someone had tried to blow up the palace for a second time. It was surreal—and it was the most precious moment she could have ever imagined.

There were hundreds of people there, all sitting in those gold-backed chairs watching a bride walk to meet her groom at the altar. Of course, they'd expected to see another bride and groom, but from the smiles on their faces, Val didn't think they minded. She certainly didn't.

Today she was marrying *her* prince.

This was her fairy tale; it was her dream come true. It was what she'd always wanted. From the bouquet in her hand to the long stretch of white satin that she walked over on her way down the aisle. The dress that Landry had said was perfect for her—the off-the-shoulder taupe-lace gown with the satin bow belt—turned out to be perfect, since Roland had donned his full Royal Seaside Navy uniform, with the white pants and the white jacket with all its gold-medal regalia.

Sam and Landry stood as her bridesmaids while her father proudly handed her over to Roland when they made it to the altar.

After the minister read his Scriptures and commenced with all the formalities, Roland turned and spoke to Val.

"Having everything that comes with being a prince means absolutely nothing to me if I can't have you by my side," he said. "You are everything I never knew I wanted and so much more. That's why we can't wait.

We love each other and we're meant to be together. My mother believed in fate and so do I. I was running for so long, only to be stopped, finally, by you."

Val had to blink repeatedly to keep the tears that had filled her eyes from falling.

"On this day, I, Prince Roland Simon DeSaunters, take you, Valora Michele Harrington, to not only be my princess, but my friend, my confidante, my partner, my wife."

She didn't know what to say, but then again, she knew just what would say it all.

"You are my knight in shining armor. The one I've dreamed about all my life. You've opened doors for me, shielded me from gossip and physical harm. You accepted my father and declared your love for me regardless of our past. You make me feel special and, more importantly, loved unconditionally."

One tear escaped and Roland lifted a white-gloved finger to wipe it away.

"I knew I loved you when we sat barefoot on the beach together. I knew I wanted to spend the rest of my life showing you my love and unmitigated support. You are all I've ever wished for. You are my prince ever after."

* * * * *

*Rafe Lawson is only driven by his music and living a
life away from the influence of his powerful father.
The woman he meets at a high-profile celebration won't
change his playboy ways. Still, Rafe is intrigued by the
stunning secret service agent who never mixes business
and pleasure. He has no choice but use his legendary
Lawson power of seduction to win over
Avery Richards...*

Read on for a sneak peek at
SURRENDER TO ME,
the next exciting installment in author Donna Hill's
THE LAWSONS OF LOUISIANA series!

He'd noticed her the moment she walked in, and it was clear,
even in an eye-popping black gown, that she was there as
more than an invited guest. He could tell by the way her
gaze covertly scanned the room, noted the exits and followed at a discreet distance from the vice president that she
was part of his security detail—secret service. He had an
image of a .22 strapped to her inner thigh.

Unlike many highbrow gatherings of politicos and the
like that were too reserved for Rafe's taste, a Lawson party
was the real deal. Full of loud laughter, louder conversations
and the music to go with it. So of course he had to get
particularly close to talk to her.

He gave her time to assess the layout before he approached.
He came alongside her. "Can I get you anything?"

She turned cinnamon-brown eyes on him, fanned by long, curved lashes. Her smile was practiced, distant, but Rafe didn't miss the rapid beat of her pulse in the dip of her throat that belied her cool exterior. Her sleek right brow rose in question as she took him in with one long glance.

"Clearly you're not one of the waitstaff," she said with a hint of amusement in her voice.

"Rafe Lawson."

Her eyes widened for a split second. "Oh, the scandalous one."

He pressed his hand to his chest dramatically. "Guilty as charged, cher, but I have perfectly reasonable explanations for everything."

Her eyes sparkled when the light hit them. "I'm sure you do, Mr. Lawson."

"So what can I get for you that won't interfere with you being on duty?"

She tensed ever so slightly.

"Trust me. I've grown up in this life. I can spot secret service a mile away. Although I must admit that you bring class to the dark suits and sunglasses."

She glanced past him to where her colleague stood near the vice president. In one fluid motion she gave a barely imperceptible lift of her chin, a quick scan of the room and said, "Nice to meet you," as she made a move to leave.

He held her bare arm. "Tell me your name," he commanded almost in her ear. He inhaled her, felt the slight shiver that gripped her.

"Avery."

Rafe released her and followed the dangerously low-cut back of her dress with his gaze until she was out of sight.

Don't miss SURRENDER TO ME
by Donna Hill, available August 2017
wherever Harlequin® Kimani Romance™
books and ebooks are sold.

Get 2 Free Books,

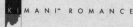

Plus 2 Free Gifts—
just for trying the Reader Service!

A love for all time

REESE RYAN

Playing
WITH
Temptation

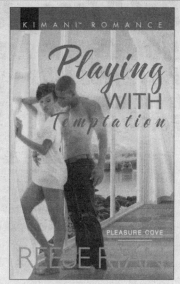

Pro football player Nate Johnston is in need of a miracle when a viral video threatens to derail his career. After breaking his heart, repairing his career is the least media consultant Kendra Williams could do. As passion smolders between them, will a jealous ex sabotage their second chance?

PLEASURE COVE

Available July 2017!

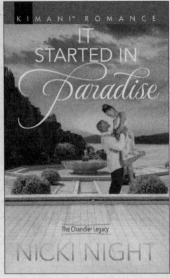

Dear Reader,

It's time for the big royal wedding! I so enjoyed writing Roland's story because throughout the first two books he's been in the background keeping his thoughts and feelings to himself. Well, Val has stepped onto the scene, and she's brought out every feeling Roland has been desperately trying to keep at bay. I love this couple so much. Neither of them imagined they would ever find someone special, and when they do, they almost still can't believe it. So it was very fitting to wrap up this trilogy with their love story. I hope you have enjoyed your time on Grand Serenity Island!

Happy reading,

ac

"You never know what people truly think about you when all they've ever heard was gossip," she admitted.

"Misjudgments," Roland commented as his eyes seemed to search her face for something she wasn't quite sure she possessed. "People tend to do that far too often."

"I agree," she said, her throat suddenly dry.

"Honesty is a beautiful thing," he continued as he rubbed his hands down his thighs.

"It can be," Val replied. "On the other hand, some people can't accept the truth as well as they can a lie."

"You want to know what's true at this very moment?" Roland asked.

Was he leaning closer?

Val clenched the napkin she'd been holding more tightly in her hand.

"What?" she asked in response.

She didn't really think she wanted to know what Roland was going to say next, but at the same time, she didn't want this moment to end.

He *was* in fact leaning closer. He'd planted a palm on the blanket to hold himself steady as his face neared hers.

"I want you," he whispered.

She gulped, loudly. Then as she licked her lips impulsively, his

"Ye